THE **NIGHT** SHE
DISAPPEARED

THE
NIGHT
SHE
DISAPPEARED

APRIL HENRY

SQUARE
FISH

HENRY HOLT AND COMPANY • NEW YORK

Thanks to Lieutenant Cameron Piner of the Guilford County Sheriff's Office for answering my questions about dive teams. And I wouldn't have met Lieutenant Piner if it weren't for Lee Lofland, a veteran police investigator who set up the Writers Police Academy. More thanks go to Robin Burcell, police investigator and author, who pretty much knows everything and is always willing to share it. As always, any mistakes are my own.

SQUARE
FISH

An imprint of Macmillan Publishing Group, LLC

Square Fish and the Square Fish logo are trademarks of Macmillan and are used by Henry Holt and Company under license from Macmillan.

Library of Congress Cataloging-in-Publication Data
Henry, April.
The night she disappeared / April Henry.
p. cm.
"Christy Ottaviano Books."
Summary: Told from various viewpoints; Gabie and Drew set out to prove that their missing co-worker Kayla is not dead, and to find her before she is, while the police search for her body and the man who abducted her.
ISBN 978-1-250-01674-4
[1. Missing persons—Fiction. 2. Kidnapping—Fiction. 3. Family problems—Fiction. 4. Oregon—Fiction. 5. Mystery and detective stories.] I. Title.
PZ7.H39356Nig 2012 [Fic]—dc23 2011030876

Originally published in the United States by
Christy Ottaviano Books/Henry Holt and Company
First Square Fish Edition: March 2013
Square Fish logo designed by Filomena Tuosto
fiercereads.com

11 13 15 17 19 20 18 16 14 12

LEXILE: HL680L

For L. K. Madigan,
a good friend and a great writer
gone too soon

THE **NIGHT** SHE **DISAPPEARED**

ORDER FORM

First Name John

Last Name Robertson

Delivery Address 1091 River Road

Apartment Number NA

Phone Number 503-555-1212

Driver's License for Credit Card / Check Orders

Cash

Size Large x 3

Kind Meat Monster

Extra

☐ Pepperoni   ☐ Black Olives   ☐ Onions

☐ Salami   ☐ Green Peppers   ☐ Pineapple

☐ Can. Bacon   ☐ Grnd. Beef   ☐ Jalapeños

☐ Linguica   ☐ It. Sausage   ☐ Anchovies

☐ Mushrooms   ☐ Tomatoes   ☐ Xtra Cheese

THE DAY IT HAPPENED

DREW

IT WAS ME who took the order. It could have been anyone. I don't know why I feel guilty. But it was me.

"Pete's Pizza. This is Drew," I said, and winked at Kayla. She blew the black bangs out of her blue eyes and smiled. Even in that stupid white baseball cap Pete makes us wear, she looked hot. I wondered if she knew that. Probably. Then Kayla picked up a handful of pepperoni. She weighed it on the small silver scale and started laying the circles out on the pizza skin. She had already put down the sauce and cheese.

"Yeah," a man said. "I'd like to order some pizzas to be delivered." There was nothing special about his voice. The cops have asked me over and over. Did he have an accent? Did he sound drunk? Calm? Angry? Was he old? Young? Did he sound like a smoker? Did I recognize his voice?

For each question, I have the same answer. *I don't know*.

I don't know, I don't know, I don't know. I haven't been able to tell them anything useful.

Each time I say that, they sigh or shake their heads and then ask me another question. Like if they ask it enough times in enough ways, I'll remember something important.

But I never do.

I pulled an order form toward me and grabbed a pen. "Okay. What kind do you want?"

"Three larges. Hey, is the girl in the Mini Cooper making deliveries tonight?"

He meant Gabie. Kayla had traded with Gabie so Kayla could get Friday off. Kayla and I were the only two on. Miguel had clocked out at seven thirty, after the dinner rush was over.

Kayla was on delivery because I don't have a car. She had only gone out once that night. It was a Wednesday, so it was slow. And it was already eight. We close at ten.

Pete's Pizza is in a little strip mall. On one side is a florist and a Starbucks and a Blockbuster. On the other is a Baskin-Robbins and a Subway. Kayla used to work at the Subway. But Pete pays fifty cents more an hour, plus extra for deliveries. And then there's tips. Kayla always got a lot of them. She always said she liked to make deliveries.

Says. She always *says* she *likes.* I shouldn't use the past tense.

Kayla says.

I thought the guy must have flirted with Gabie the last time she delivered a pizza to him. Jealousy pinched me. It wasn't like I was dating Gabie. We just worked together. I wasn't dating anyone. But this guy, this guy felt confident enough to flirt with the pizza delivery girl. He could probably stand behind a cute girl in a movie line and when he got to the window he'd be buying tickets for them both.

I didn't answer him directly when he asked about Gabie. Instead I just said, "One of our staff members will deliver your order in forty-five minutes."

The fact that he asked about Gabie is the only thing I've been able to tell the cops, but it doesn't help. Gabie hasn't been able to tell them anything either.

"So what kind do you want?" I asked.

"Three Meat Monsters."

Meat Monsters are gross. They have sausage, pepperoni, ground beef, and linguica. After you eat a slice, your lips feel slick. And if you look in the mirror later, you'll find an orange ring around your mouth. Even if you use a napkin.

He told me his name was John Robertson. He gave me his phone number and his address. I told him it would cost $35.97 and hung up the phone.

"Order in!" I joked, like it was a busy night. Then I grabbed three pizza skins from the cooler. Kayla and I got to work. We stood hip to hip, not working fast, but not slow, either. Just a steady, comfortable rhythm. We've worked together enough that we didn't have to say much about who was going to do what. At one point we both reached for the Alpo—otherwise known as sausage— and our hands touched. We looked at each other and kind of smiled. Then I pulled my hand back and let her go first.

I think about that a lot now.

Was I the last friendly, normal person to touch her?

TRANSCRIPT OF 911 CALL

911 Operator: 911. Police, fire, or medical?

Drew Lyle: Um, police.

911 Operator: What seems to be the problem?

Drew Lyle: I, uh, I work at Pete's Pizza. And my coworker went to deliver some pizzas, and she hasn't come back, and she doesn't answer her cell.

911 Operator: What time did she leave?

Drew Lyle: Around 8:45.

911 Operator: This evening?

Drew Lyle: Yeah. Only, she hasn't come back. She should have been back here at least an hour ago.

911 Operator: Okay, sir, we're dispatching an officer to your location.

THE SECOND DAY

GABIE

BEFORE SCHOOL STARTS Thursday, Drew comes up to my locker, which is weird. We both go to Wilson. We get along okay at work, but we're not really friends at school.

"Gabie," he says, and then for a minute he doesn't say anything else. He looks terrible. His eyes are like two bruises, and his sun-streaked hair is even messier than usual. I wonder if he's been out partying and never went to bed. Finally, he says, "Did you hear about what happened to Kayla last night?"

It sounds bad. "No. What?" Kayla asked to switch nights with me. Maybe she cut herself slicing Canadian bacon on the Hobart. Pete's always after us to cut the meat thinner so we can weigh it out to the microgram. Three ounces on a small, no more, no less. Pete doesn't cheat anyone, but he doesn't give anything away, either. And when you use the Hobart, you have more control if you don't use the metal pusher part. The part that protects your fingers.

"Kayla went to deliver a pizza, and she never came back." He bites his lip and looks up at the ceiling. His gray eyes fill with tears. It surprises me so much that for a minute I don't take in what he said. Drew Lyle. Crying. I didn't think he really cared about anything.

And then it sinks in. *Kayla didn't come back?* Pressure fills my chest, making it hard to breathe. "What did you do?"

"After close, I kept waiting for her. You know, Kayla doesn't even have a key, and her backpack was in the break room. I called her cell a bunch, but no one answered."

I imagine Kayla running a red light or a drunk driver plowing into her. "So she was in an accident?"

Drew shakes his head. "No. I mean, I don't know. Right now, nobody knows. She never came back. She just disappeared."

Could Kayla have run away? For about one second, I consider the idea. But Kayla has a lot going for her, probably more than most people. This fall, she'll be heading to Oregon State on a softball scholarship. Even before she broke up with her boyfriend, Brock, lots of guys would come in and buy a slice just so they could talk to her. So I figure it's not like she's lonely. She didn't tell me why she wanted Friday night off, but I thought maybe there was a new boyfriend.

Besides, if you were going to run away from your life, wouldn't you just call in sick to work and then drive off into the sunset? Why go through all the trouble of pretending to make a pizza delivery?

So what happened to her? Then I remember a news story from a few years back. "Maybe she swerved or something and rolled the car down a steep hill like that one girl did up in Washington a couple of years ago," I tell Drew. "You know, like maybe Kayla's in a ditch, but no one can see her car from the road."

Drew blinks, and a single tear runs down his face. This can't be real. I can't be watching Drew Lyle cry. By now, it's like we're in a little bubble. I no longer see the kids hurrying past us or spinning their locker combinations and reaching in to yank out their books. I only have eyes for Drew, his long nose that bends to the right at the tip, his teeth that press into his lower lip, and his silver eyes welling up with tears.

"The police don't think so. The phone number the guy called from, it turned out, was really a pay phone miles from where he said he wanted the pizzas delivered." Drew makes a sound like a laugh. "He must have found the last pay phone in Portland. And the address he gave me—there's a real street called that, but the houses are like a mile apart, and none of them have that number." He takes a deep, shuddering breath. "The police think Kayla might have been kidnapped. Or worse."

Does he mean, like, dead? I try to picture it, but something inside me just says *no way*. Kayla's always goofing around, laughing, dancing, bumping hips with whoever's working next to her, taking up more space in the kitchen area than I ever will. Her last name's Cutler, but she looks like it should be O'Shaugnnessy—black hair, huge blue eyes, skin as pale as milk. She's pretty, so pretty she could be a model. Everybody always says so.

Maybe that's why they took her. I'm suddenly glad for my dirty blond hair and my face that still breaks out even though I'm seventeen.

"So have they asked for a ransom?" I ask.

Drew shakes his head again. "No. Pete stayed there all night in case they called. But nobody did. And the kidnapper hasn't contacted her parents either." While I'm still taking all this in, he touches my shoulder. "There's something else I wanted to talk to you about before the police did."

"What?" I wonder if he wants me to lie for him. Not tell about him and Kayla smoking weed in the cooler that one time.

"They asked for you first," Drew says, interrupting my thoughts. "The guy who called asked if the girl in the Mini Cooper was delivering."

When Your Child Is Missing: A Family Survival Guide

U.S. DEPARTMENT OF JUSTICE

One of the most critical aspects in the search for a missing child is the gathering of evidence that may hold clues about a child's disappearance or whereabouts. The mishandling of evidence can adversely affect an investigation. Similarly, the collection and preservation of evidence are key to finding a missing child. Parents play a vital role by protecting evidence in and around the home, and by gathering information about persons or situations that might hold clues. Following are some tips on what you should do to help law enforcement conduct a thorough and complete investigation.

Secure your child's room. Even though your child may have disappeared from outside the home, your child's room should be searched thoroughly by law enforcement for clues and evidence. Don't clean the child's room, wash your child's clothes, or pick up your house. Don't allow well-meaning family members or friends to disturb anything. Even a trash bin or a computer may contain clues that lead to the recovery of the child.

Do not touch or remove anything from your child's room or from your home that might have your child's fingerprints, DNA, or scent on it. This includes your child's hairbrush, bed linens, worn clothing, pencil with bite marks, diary, or address book. With a good set of fingerprints or a sample of DNA from hair, law enforcement may be able to tell whether your child has been in a particular car or house. With good scent material, tracking dogs may be able to find your child.

THE SECOND DAY

TODD AND JEREMY

IT'S SO STUPID, but you can't buy fireworks in Oregon, or even have them in your possession. At least, nothing that's any good. Nothing that goes more than six feet along the ground or twelve inches into the air. Which pretty much leaves those black tablets that grow into ash snakes after you light them.

Oh, and sparklers. Lame-o.

Say you still want showers of sparks, cascades of shimmering color, bottle rockets and M-80s, Monkeys Violating Heaven, Assault Choppers, Alien Abductions, or Barracuda Fountains. Then you have to cross the state line to Vancouver, Washington, around the Fourth of July or New Year's. You have to find a stand that doesn't care about your out-of-state plates and just hope the occasional police sting doesn't nab you once you're back on the other side of the river. And if you're smart, you buy enough fireworks to last all year—not only for the Fourth of July, but also for New Year's and Labor Day and just screwing around.

Which is what Todd and Jeremy are doing. Messing

around. They have two six-packs of beer on the floor-boards and they've already decided to blow off school tomorrow. They'll drive out by the industrial section next to the river, where at night there will be no witnesses. No one to pick up the phone and tattle. No one to fret that a spark will land on the roof of their McMansion.

Everything is dark and quiet. Except for one thing. A little light shines dimly to their right, closer to the river. Without discussing it, Jeremy turns the wheel. The pickup follows the narrow track that leads toward the light. If it hadn't been night, if they hadn't been on that empty road, Jeremy and Todd wouldn't have seen it.

In the headlights of the truck, this is what they see: a red Ford Taurus. On top is a plastic triangular sign, like a taxicab's, that reads PETE'S PIZZA—FREE DELIVERY with a phone number. The driver's door is open, and they can see inside. The overhead light is on. A black leather purse rests on the passenger seat. The keys dangle from the ignition. But there is no one in the car.

And scattered on the ground are three pizza boxes and a white baseball cap.

FOUND ON KAYLA'S DRESSER

FORTUNE COOKIE MESSAGE:

You are about to embark on a most delightful journey.

THE THIRD DAY

GABIE

I'M IN ADVANCED ENGLISH when my name comes over the loudspeaker. "Gabie Klug, Gabie Klug, please report to the office."

Someone in the back of the room says "ooooh!" like I'm in big trouble, but it's more like they're mocking me. I've never gotten in trouble for anything.

I'm glad Drew warned me yesterday. I would have been so freaked out to be called from class to see a cop standing in the office. He's about the same age as my parents. He even wears a uniform like they do, except theirs are surgeon's scrubs. And of course, neither of them would ever wear a black gun in a holster.

If Drew hadn't warned me, I would probably think something had gone wrong at the hospital, maybe a crazed patient had taken my parents hostage and demanded a heart transplant, stat.

The cop tells me to go into a little conference room off the main office. Kathy, the secretary, doesn't take her eyes off us. She looks like she would give anything to follow us right in.

"I'm Sergeant Thayer," he tells me, taking out a notebook. "And you're Gabie Klug?" He pronounces it wrong, so that it rhymes with *glug*. Which is kind of annoying, because he just heard Kathy say it over the loudspeaker.

"It's like *clue* with a hard *g* on the end. Klug," I tell him. "Have you found Kayla?" I want to know but am scared to hear the answer.

"Not yet. But we did locate her car last night. In an industrial area down by the Willamette River."

"So it was just parked down there? Did she have a flat tire or something?" Maybe Kayla went off to try to find a gas station.

"No." Sergeant Thayer looks grim. "The car's mechanical condition seems fine. The keys were in the ignition, and her purse was on the seat. But the door was open, and there were pizza boxes scattered on the ground."

It takes me a minute to figure it out. "So somebody took her? Like, kidnapped her?"

"It looks that way."

I start to tremble, imagining what happened to Kayla after that. "But they really wanted me. They had asked for me."

Sergeant Thayer screws up his face. "Who told you that?"

"Drew."

"Well, we have to look at the facts here, Gabie. And the facts show that Kayla was the one who this guy targeted, no matter what Drew thinks he heard on the phone. She set her emergency brake, which she wouldn't have had time to do if she were in a panic. She left her purse on the seat and her keys in the ignition. Are those the actions of a girl who is afraid? Of a girl who sees a stranger outside her car?" He answers his own question. "No. We think Kayla was stopped by someone she knew. She got out of the car and then he forced her to leave with him. Maybe he didn't know Kayla that well, but we believe he *did* know her. And that she knew him. Has she talked about anyone making her nervous, another student or even a customer?" He steeples his fingers and looks at me over them. I can see his impatience in how he taps his index fingers together.

"Kayla didn't exactly confide in me. We just knew each other from work. We didn't hang out or anything."

He continues as if I haven't said anything. "Maybe even a couple of guys together?"

"No. She never said anything. And she never acted like anyone made her nervous." Kayla always seems to have a good time at work. The truth is, I always like working with her. Sure, it's still work, but she makes it fun, too. I kind of wish Kayla was my friend. But even though she's always nice to me, she already has a bunch of friends at school.

"Now, we understand from your boss that you switched schedules with Kayla so that she worked on Wednesday when you normally would have. Whose idea was that?" His eyes drill into me.

I feel guilty, even though it wasn't my idea. "Kayla wanted Friday off. I was fine with it, because I didn't have plans." Which is an understatement.

He makes another note. "So she was going on a date?"

"She didn't say, but I thought she was." Kayla had

pursed her lips and smiled after she asked me if I could do her a "big, big favor." Looking like she had a happy secret.

"Then you don't know who she was going to go out with?" Sergeant Thayer raps out. "Do you have any guesses?"

"Half the school and half our customers wouldn't mind dating Kayla Cutler," I say. I'm still trying to take it in. The pizza boxes scattered on the ground. The car door open, but nobody there. I try to think of Kayla dead. But it's impossible. I can see her in my mind's eye, make her tip her head back while she laughs, hear her humming an old Green Day song, see her bend down to get something from the cooler while half the customers appreciatively watch her butt. If you stand right next to her making pizzas, mixed with the smell of tomato sauce and pepperoni is Kayla's own faint scent, a sweet smell like vanilla.

I knew Kayla a little from school, but it was only at Pete's that I really got to know her. You can't help but know Kayla. She talks nonstop. Not just about herself. She also wants to know about you.

"So is it true what I heard—that you're going to Stanford?" she asked me one slow Saturday afternoon. It was too late for the latest lunch and too early for even old people to eat dinner.

"Yeah." I duck my head.

"I hear so many people apply there that they take the stack of admission forms and throw them down a flight of stairs," she says. "And they only look at the ones who make it to the bottom."

I can't tell if Kayla really believes that, but it makes as much sense as anything. I shrug.

"And major in premed?"

"I guess."

Kayla tilts her head. "You don't sound really excited."

"It's just that I'm not sure I want to be a doctor."

"Because of all the blood and guts? You're a vegetarian, right?"

"That's not it." I'm surprised she remembers. "It's more that my parents are surgeons, and that's their whole life. They don't have room for much else. I'd like to design stuff, like the things we use every day, you know, like forks and light switches, but my parents say that's not a real job."

Her brows pull together. "Why not?"

"I guess they don't want me to be a starving artist. They say I could always make stuff on the side."

She looks skeptical. "While going to medical school? I'll bet there's not any time on the side for years and years. How long do you have to go to school for, anyway?"

"Four years to get your undergrad, then four of med school, and then at least two years as a resident."

"Ten more years?" Grinning, Kayla shook her head. It was clear that she wanted to be someplace real in ten years, not just starting out.

But now what? She must be dead, or she will be soon. That's what happens when a girl gets taken. Maybe her body is already in a shallow mountain grave. Isn't that what they always call it in the paper? *A shallow mountain grave.* Kayla won't be laughing or humming anymore. And her smell will be of something else.

Only I don't believe she's dead. Something inside of me says *No.* But that's just stupid. I hear my mother's voice. *It's irrational.* The greatest sin, in my parents' eyes—being irrational. Of course Kayla is dead. She must be.

The shaking is getting harder. My arms are trembling no matter how hard I squeeze my hands together. Sergeant Thayer's eyes bore into me.

"What about Brock Chambers? We understand Kayla had recently broken up with him. Do you know if he was angry about that?"

"Brock? I just know who he is, that's all. I've never even talked to him. Kayla didn't seem like she was upset or worried or anything, though."

Sergeant Thayer asks me a few more questions, but it's clear I don't know anything, and it's also clear he's getting frustrated.

When I walk back into class, everyone stares at me.

And I keep thinking about what Drew said. About how the guy asked for me. It should have been me, down by the river. It should have been my purse on the seat, my hat on the ground. He wanted me. I don't care what Sergeant Thayer said. This guy wanted me. The girl in the Mini Cooper. He wanted me first.

Maybe he still wants me.

FOUND ON KAYLA'S DRESSER

<u>TO DO</u>

NO MORE CHOCOLATE!

Call Sami

Get pink streaks?

Drink more water

Buy extra-long sheets for dorm

Practice guitar

DON'T WORRY IF PEOPLE
THINK YOU'RE A NUT

Sign up for 10k

Practice French

EVIDENCE

PORTLAND POLICE		Property class:
☒ Evidence ☐ Found ☐ Inmate ☐ Safekeeping ☐ Destroy		

Case number: CTO-Q 5-11 169	Badge number: 431295	Initials: RB
Date of Collection: MAY 9	Time of Collection: 1:32 p.m.	Collected by: RANDALL BOYD

Description of Evidence:	BLOODY ROCK

Location of Evidence:	BANK OF WILLAMETTE RIVER, 200 YARDS FROM KAYLA CUTLER'S CAR

PORTLAND POLICE		Property class:
☒ Evidence ☐ Found ☐ Inmate ☐ Safekeeping ☐ Destroy		

Case number: CTO-Q 5-11 169	Badge number: 431295	Initials: RB
Date of Collection: MAY 9	Time of Collection: 3:47 p.m.	Collected by: RANDALL BOYD

Description of Evidence:	TOOTHBRUSH FOR DNA TESTING

Location of Evidence:	KAYLA CUTLER'S BEDROOM

THE THIRD DAY

GAVIN

EYES OPEN, EYES CLOSED. It doesn't matter. This is a black dive. With his bare fingers, Gavin sifts through mud and silt as he crawls along the bottom of the Willamette River, looking for Kayla Cutler's body.

People don't understand if you tell them there is no visibility at the bottom. They picture scuba divers in the ocean surrounded by schools of colorful fish. They still think you can see your hand if you hold it in front of your face.

No. You can see nothing. Carry a powerful dive light, and you can't see its beam even if you place it in front of your mask.

In the blackest black, Gavin is deprived of every sense except touch. His entire body has become a giant eye as his mind connects his fingertips, toes, and everything in between to create a picture of what he is touching.

Sometimes the touch is horrifying. He still remembers the feel of a human hand against his throat as he searched the murky depths of Blue Lake in 1999. He had finned directly into the outstretched arm of a dead six-year-old girl. She had drowned at a church picnic.

Gavin is part of the Multnomah County dive team, which is called out a couple of times a month. Drownings, suicides, murders, missing persons, vehicle crashes, dumped vehicles, evidence searches, and the occasional Homeland Security directive.

But most of it involves people. He has lost track of how many bodies he has recovered in the last eleven years. A baby thrown from a bridge. An old man who took his last fishing trip. Airplane crashes; those are the worst. The bodies shattered beyond belief—missing arms, legs, heads. And then there are the suicides who jump from one of Portland's eleven bridges. From fifteen stories up, the height of the Fremont bridge, the water is rock hard. The impact rips off clothes and blasts leg bones up into the torso.

Sometimes the team looks for evidence instead of people. On his last dive, Gavin used an underwater metal detector to find a chrome .357 handgun that had killed a clerk at a Deliteful Donuts. Even with the detector, it took four hours. Once he located the gun, Gavin sealed it in a watertight container with the barrel pointing up. The gun stayed in the water until it went to the crime lab, where it was dried and processed. A lot of people think fingerprints and gunpowder residue will be washed away by water.

This is a myth, as the man who is now facing murder charges has learned.

Right now, pawing the darkness, Gavin doesn't know

where the shore is, where he himself is, where he has been, or where he is going.

That's why Gavin has Jack, his tender. Unlike Gavin, Jack can see where Gavin is and where he is going by watching his bubbles, the angle of his line against shore landmarks, and how the line moves. Next to Jack, the backup tender is drawing every move Gavin makes, creating an underwater map showing obstructions and entanglement risks, as well as what areas have been searched. And in an emergency, it will also show Gavin's last known location.

Gavin's line is secured to a post driven into the riverbank, and Jack controls him with a series of tugs and jerks. These signals are their only form of communication, orientation, safety. Through the line, Jack can tell him to go up or down, left or right, or ask if he is okay. And Gavin can tell Jack if he is entangled but okay, okay but needs assistance, or, if worst comes to worst, in immediate danger. Some dive teams only have one signal for trouble. Which is just asking for trouble, in Gavin's opinion.

Jack has adjusted the girth strap so that Gavin can still breathe, but it's tight enough that he feels every twitch. The tether point is slightly off center to keep the line from going between his legs. All Gavin's gear is trim, nothing dangling. Entanglement is the number one cause of death in this line of work. He has his quick-release pony bottle and shears and wire cutters. Knives might puncture him, his equipment, or the body.

Gavin has two jobs: to search for Kayla's body and to

maintain a taut line. If he feels slack, it means Jack wants him to go farther out. If Jack wants Gavin to come back, he'll reel him in.

Besides the backup tender, there is also a backup diver and a 90-percent-ready diver. Rather than sending all three divers into the water, where they would face the same risk of entanglement, entrapment, or just plain fatigue, it's far better to have warm, rested, and ready-to-go divers with full tanks.

Gavin pats and paws, his fingers translating what he touches into images. Stones, a branch, gravel, mud, an old tire. In other words, nothing. Jack pulls him in another two feet and he starts over. Dives are exhausting, using up every bit of physical and mental energy. Gavin thinks about the girl they're looking for. He saw her picture in the paper. And he knows they found a bloody rock right at the edge of the river, the bank all torn up. It looks like she struggled, the attacker hit her, possibly raped her, dumped her in the river, and she died. None of those things necessarily in that order.

So what they are looking for is a body. Earlier, they had the cadaver dogs out in boats, but they didn't alert to anything. The body could have been pushed far downstream, or it could be caught on a strainer—brush or a fallen tree that traps debris while letting the water rush through. If that happened, Gavin hopes the girl was dead long before she reached it. Otherwise, the water pressure would hold her in place against the strainer until she slowly drowned.

With luck, the body is still on the bottom within reach. It takes a week or longer for a floater to pop up.

Underwater, a body has an effective weight of about five pounds. If he finds her, she'll still be easy to maneuver, at least until he gets her into the air.

The worst thing is that the parents are on shore and have refused to leave. If Gavin doesn't find anything, they won't understand. Won't understand that it's like searching on your hands and knees—blindfolded. You can pass by something two inches away and never know you missed it. Besides, in a fast-water environment like this one—made worse by recent heavy rains—the girl is probably long gone. Miles downriver. Washed out to the ocean. Unless she got snagged on something.

And if Gavin does find this girl? That will be worse. The parents screaming and tearing at their hair as he drags what was once their baby onshore.

But at least they'll have an answer.

THE THIRD DAY

GABIE

"YOU'RE NOT GOING to work," my mom says when I come downstairs wearing my red polo shirt with PETE'S PIZZA embroidered on the left side. Her tone is halfway between a question and a command. The kitchen counters are covered with black cloth grocery bags from New Seasons.

"I have to. I'm on the schedule for today."

"No one will be expecting you to go in. Not after what happened." She slides a gallon of organic skim milk into the refrigerator, and then another.

"I can't just sit around here thinking. I'd rather be busy and keep my mind off it."

She plucks two green cardboard cartons filled with tiny strawberries from the top of a bag. "How can you keep your mind off it when you're going to be right where it happened?"

"But it didn't happen at Pete's," I tell her as she carefully washes one strawberry, pulls off the green cap, and pops it in her mouth. "It happened down by the river.

Miles away." Mom doesn't know that the guy asked for me first. She doesn't know because I haven't told her.

Mom and Dad don't even know that I deliver pizzas. The car sign attaches with magnets, and there's two signs in the storeroom at work. Well, one I guess, since the police probably kept the one that was on Kayla's car.

My parents are all about avoiding risks. The key doesn't get turned in the car's ignition until all the seat belts are buckled. Even though they live on their cell phones, my parents never answer them when they're driving. And don't even think about riding a bike without a helmet. I got the condom lecture when I was thirteen, and Mom kept talking, even though I begged her to stop. I'm expected to eat at least seven servings of fruit and vegetables a day, plus three glasses of skim milk. The few times there's ice cream in the freezer, it's always reduced fat, and the "butter" in the fridge is something made with an ingredient from pine trees to lower cholesterol.

Being careful is a great way to run an operating room. But I'm not so sure about life.

"I don't know." Mom picks up an empty bag, revealing a long smear of scarlet on the pale gray granite counter. She clucks her tongue and grabs a sponge. A strawberry must have gotten stuck underneath the bag. It looks like blood.

I wonder where Kayla is now. She must be dead. But I can't make myself believe that. Something inside of me still says *no*.

My parents believe in being responsible, so I say, "Pete called me during lunch period to make sure I'm coming to work. He says they really need me. They're asking extra people to work, it's so busy. So it will be safe." I take a deep breath. "Come on—I want to be around other people. If I stay home, I'll just sit around and lose my mind."

Mom purses her lips. "How about if I take you to work and your dad picks you up?"

"But if you guys get called into surgery, I'll be stuck at Pete's without a ride home," I point out. "It's better if I take the Mini."

The only reason they let me have the Mini was because it had good ratings for head injuries, "thoracic trauma," and risk of rollover. Plus I had to promise that I would never drink before driving it, never transport more than one friend, and never speed.

"This goes against my better judgment," Mom finally says, "but all right. Be sure and keep your phone on. Text me when you get there and when you leave."

"Thank you!" I give her a hug. It's only when she hugs me back that I feel how hard it is for her to let me go. She runs her fingers along my shoulder blades and takes a sniff of my hair before she finally releases me.

SERGEANT THAYER is sitting right outside the front door of Pete's in an unmarked cop car. The car is one of those nondescript brown four-door Fords with a light bolted next to the driver's-side mirror and a short antenna sticking up from the trunk.

It might as well be painted blue and white and have a light bar on the top.

He's watching the front door with a notebook in his hand. And there's a lot to look at. A line of people spills out the door and winds all the way past the front windows. I've never seen this many people at Pete's, not even on Super Bowl Sunday. Flyers have been taped up in every window. All I can see is a photo and a block of words, but I know they must be asking for people's help in finding Kayla.

I go around back to park, then use the employee door. After putting my purse in a cubby, I grab a baseball cap and apron from the boxes in the break room. No one's there because it's so busy. When I walk out into the kitchen area, pepperoni pieces and cheese shreds dot the black and white floor. Pete does not believe in waste, so that's almost as big a surprise as the people waiting in line.

Pete's wife, Sonya, who normally just does the books at their house, and sometimes works delivery, slams the cash drawer closed with one hip while at the same time counting out some guy's change. Drew, Courtney, and Pete are making pizzas. Pete's hands are a blur as he scatters mushrooms with one hand and black olives with the other. And he's not using the scale—another first.

"Where do you want me?" I ask Pete. "On the register or here?"

At the sound of my voice, Drew turns and smiles, one side of his mouth lifting higher than the other. Then he grabs a wooden paddle and opens the oven door. I tell myself it's the five-hundred-degree ovens that make my cheeks get hot.

Pete's hands never stop moving. "Help Sonya until we get caught up with orders."

I go to the front and grab a pad and pen. "Who's next?"

A girl with frizzy red hair, wearing a tie-dye shirt, says, "I think I am."

"What would you like?"

Instead of answering, she says, "So this is where she worked, right? Kayla?"

"Yeah," I say, biting off the word and not making eye contact. Maybe my mom was right. Maybe I shouldn't have come to work.

"So have you heard anything? Anything at all?"

"No. What would you like to order?"

"I guess a slice of cheese."

"Anything to drink?" I know that she's going to say no even before she shakes her head.

That's how it goes for the next couple of hours. A lot of questions, a lot of orders for plain slices and pepperoni slices. It's like the price of admission to gawk at what isn't a crime scene. I recognize a couple dozen kids from school, but there are a lot of adults too, who look around as if they're going to find her picture hanging on the wall, or who ask me questions about what Kayla's like. As much as possible, I answer every question with a single word. Or, when I can, with even less. Maybe just a look to remind them that Kayla isn't an abstraction to us, that Kayla is real.

The only break in the evening is when Pete sends Courtney up so that Sonya can go to the bathroom. Courtney really tries to answer all the questions about Kayla, which only results in people asking more questions and not actually getting around to ordering pizza. I hear one customer say, "Do you think it could have been her boyfriend?"

But instead of answering, Courtney walks away, her fingers untying her apron strings as she goes up to Pete. Tears are sliding down her face. "I can't do this, Pete, I just can't." She balls up her apron, and he takes it like he doesn't know what it is.

"Go home, take some time, get your head together," he says, but he looks kind of desperate. We're barely keeping up as it is. And I get the feeling that Courtney doesn't mean she can't do this just tonight. I think she just quit.

"What would you like?" I say to the tall guy at the counter. He's not quite as old as my dad, but close. He's wearing a Yankees baseball cap and a Trailblazers jersey, but he's overweight enough that you know the only exercise he gets is yelling at the TV.

"That depends," he says, leaning forward. "What are you offering?" He raises one eyebrow and gives me a sleazy smile.

I blink. Am I going crazy, or did he just say that? The fine hairs on my arms rise up. "Get out!" I say, raising one arm and pointing.

The woman standing behind him shakes her finger. "You heard the girl!"

Everyone is looking at him, but he still stands with that sick, silly grin.

"Just get the hell out of here!" I spit the words at him. It's not until he's gone that I start to shake.

TRANSCRIPT OF 911 CALL

911 Operator: 911. Police, fire, or medical?

Alice Russo: Police.

911 Operator: What seems to be the problem?

Alice Russo: I saw a truck out where that girl disappeared. That pizza girl.

911 Operator: Do you mean Kayla Cutler?

Alice Russo: Yeah. The pizza girl.

911 Operator: What day was this, ma'am?

Alice Russo: Wednesday. Yeah, it was Wednesday. The night that girl disappeared. I saw a white pickup, like an older Toyota pickup. And it was driving real slow. They must have been looking for that girl.

911 Operator: You said "they." Was there more than one person in the pickup?

Alice Russo: I don't know. I couldn't see inside the cab. But I do know it was an older Toyota pickup. White. And I've never seen it in my neighborhood before.

THE FOURTH DAY

KAYLA

I WAKE UP. At least I think I'm awake.

Maybe I'm dead.

It's completely black. The right side of my head throbs.

I must be alive. The dead don't feel pain, do they?

Finally, after five minutes or maybe an hour, I push myself up. Big mistake. The side of my head was stuck to whatever I was lying on. By the time I figure that out, it's too late. The pain makes me shriek. It's like someone just tried to scalp me.

I keep shrieking, only now I find words. "Help me! Somebody help me! I'm hurt!"

The words come right back to me. My shouts feel trapped in here, wherever *here* is. Just like I am. What happened? Where am I?

Nobody comes. Nobody shouts back.

A warm trickle of blood curves down my neck. How bad is it? I'm scared to know. If I put my hand up, will I touch bone? Maybe even my brain?

My breathing speeds up. I hear myself whimpering, a fast, soft sound that scares me even more.

Finally, I take a deep breath and put my fingertips up to the side of my head. The cut feels obscenely like parted lips. It runs from my temple to just above my ear. It's bleeding slowly, but not gushing. No splinters of bone. Nothing that feels like brain. I take my hand away.

Blindly, I reach out and pat the space around me. I'm sitting on something that feels like a bed. Behind me is a wall. To the left is another wall. I stand up and almost immediately discover a third wall that runs parallel to the bed. I run my fingers along the walls and eventually find the familiar shape of a light switch.

The light—which comes from two buzzing fluorescent tubes—is so bright that I have to close my eyes. I force them open.

The air sparkles with white confetti. Dizzy.

I close my eyes and sit down. Hard. My stomach rises like I'm going to puke. I manage to swallow it back.

When I'm finally able to open my eyes again, I look around.

What is this place? Where am I?

It's just one room, about eight by fourteen feet, most of it taken up with the navy blue futon twin bed I'm sitting on. No windows. The walls are plain white. The ceiling is a little over six feet high, which means it's too short. The whole thing is claustrophobic.

At the foot of the bed is a short white bookcase with a small TV on top. And past that there's a toilet in one corner and a door in the other.

A door!

I rush to it. Or at least I start to. I take two steps. Then the dizziness overwhelms me. I fall to my knees, but I still keep moving, ignoring the blood that freckles the floor. I have to get out of here.

But the handle won't turn more than a half inch. I twist it the other way. It won't move at all.

"Let me out! Let me out!" I pound on the door. Then I stop to listen.

Nothing.

Silence.

No one is coming. Maybe no one is even listening.

"Help me! Help me! I'm alive! I'm alive, and I'm in here."

Holding on to the doorknob, I manage to pull myself to my feet. I kick at the door, as close as I can get to the handle, hoping to pop the lock. It doesn't budge. I kick and pound and yell. The white door is smudged with rusty fingerprints from where I touched my head. I fall down and get back up. Again. And again. I cry and scream until I'm sick, dry heaving, strings of bile hanging from my lips. But as soon as I stop gagging, I start banging on the door again, shouting and calling.

Finally, I have to lie down. I press my face next to the crack at the bottom of the door. It's dark on the other side, like there's nothing and no one there. Like I'm sealed away in a tomb.

"Let me out," I say, but now it's a whisper. "Let me out."

THE FOURTH DAY

"JOHN ROBERTSON"

THE SCREAMS RISE again from the special room I built. Faint but still audible. I set down my X-Acto Number 11, pick up the TV clicker, and press the plus sign on the volume button. There. That takes care of that.

Only it doesn't. Not really.

Things are not going according to plan. Didn't I learn anything last time? But no, I was too eager. Again.

Four days ago, all my plans were supposed to come to fruition. It was a moonless night. Moonless meant it would be hard for the pizza delivery person to figure out that the address I had given didn't exist. Difficult for the few neighbors to notice anything on a road without street-lights. And it was a Wednesday, which meant it would be quiet. It also meant Gabie Klug would be the one making deliveries.

Gabie is the one I chose for what I'm calling the Project. The Project, Part Two. She can be shy, but eventually she warms up and jokes with you. But only after carefully watching your face and figuring out if that's okay. If that's what you want.

She would be perfect.

Once I figured out that it was possible to get a girl to deliver herself right to me, it took me months to figure out which one I wanted. Months of greasy single slices, takeout orders, and watching the parking lot to see who made deliveries. Nine women and girls work at Pete's Pizza. But not all of them make deliveries. And of those who do? Well, take Pete's wife, Sonya. Forty, too much makeup, too much sass, too much ass. Not my type. Not my type at all. Or Courtney, with her small, hard eyes rimmed with black eye liner? Amber, with her harsh bray of a laugh?

Most are unsuitable.

My work has taught me that if you want something done right, you start with the correct raw materials. You don't begin with the wrong components and try to force them to be something they never were and never could be.

I learned that lesson again with the first girl. What was her name? Jenny? Jessica? Janie? I no longer remember. She was an experiment, that's all. It wasn't until I acquired her that I figured out she was all wrong for my purposes. It was much like when I was trying to decide between polyurethane and expanded polystyrene foam for modeling. You have to work with the expanded polystyrene before you realize it does not allow for as many finish techniques.

And Kayla? Kayla is wrong in so many ways. Angry when Gabie would be sweet. Defiant when Gabie would be submissive. Ungrateful, damaged, dirty, disgusting. Gabie will be none of those things.

When I saw the red Taurus with the lighted sign for

Pete's Pizza on top, instead of the black Mini Cooper, I knew something had gone awry. I should have driven away. It would have taken time, but I could have found a new isolated location where I could phone in a false address on another Wednesday night.

But I let my hunger overcome my good sense. I told myself that Kayla, while not perfect, could still be molded. After all, even Gabie couldn't last forever. I ignored the little voice that told me I was making a mistake, and I waved Kayla down.

When she saw my familiar face, she smiled, and I almost thought I had done the right thing. A few seconds later, I realized how wrong I was, but it was too late.

What I want—need—is to start over. With Gabie, the one I really wanted. But to do that, first I need to get rid of my mistake.

I can take Kayla down to the river and let her go. Release her from her troubles. They might not ever find her, and even if they do, the water should wash away any trace evidence. They'll never know she was alive for a few days before she went in.

And then I can start fresh.

THE FOURTH DAY

DREW

THERE'S A MANDATORY meeting in the dough room at ten this morning. We have to have it there because the break room can only hold about three people.

The room's buzzing. The conveyor belt has been turned off. Someone has dragged in chairs from the restaurant tables to supplement the folding ones. They're lined up three across down the long narrow room.

There's all kinds of rumors. Someone tried to break into Kayla's parents' house. Last night, a pizza driver from Papa John's disappeared. The cops want all the guys who work at Pete's to dress like girls and deliver pizzas as bait. Someone saw Kayla walking down Pine Street in Seattle. Pete is going to shut down and declare bankruptcy.

I just listen. It's clear nobody knows anything.

Gabie stands in the doorway a second. Then she takes the chair next to me. No one else is sitting near me. Maybe I'm being paranoid, but is it because I let Kayla go out on the delivery? Because I took the guy's order like it was real and let her drive off?

It was so crazy last night—especially after Courtney

quit—that Gabie and I didn't have a chance to talk. I was going to offer to walk her to her car, but Pete did before I could say anything.

Even though Gabie wasn't there Wednesday, I think she understands how I feel. After all, she was supposed to be working. And the guy asked for her. Me? I was the last one to see Kayla, but I can't even remember her last words. They were probably something ordinary, but now they seem important.

If only I could remember what they were.

Of course, Kayla's last words probably weren't whatever she said to me as she picked up her keys and the three red insulated boxes. And they probably weren't words at all, but a scream.

Thoughts like these are the reason I'm not sleeping anymore.

Gabie sits with her shoulder curled over, chewing on the edge of one fingernail, with her hair falling in her eyes. Her legs are jigging up and down. I have a feeling I'm not the only one who isn't sleeping. Maybe I shouldn't have told her what the guy said. But how could I not? Besides, the cops probably told her first thing.

Pete comes in. He's a little guy, about five foot five, with black hair, a big nose, and a belly. Behind him is one of the cops who talked and talked to me. At the sight of his uniform and the black gun on his hip, the room goes completely quiet.

"This is Sergeant Thayer," Pete says. "He's here to answer your questions."

Beside me, Gabie takes a deep breath. She raises her hand. "Have you found Kayla?"

"Not yet, Gabriella." A jolt of electricity goes through the room. Everyone realizes this cop knows her name. "We still don't know exactly what happened. We know some guy called in a pizza order to an address that doesn't exist. We found Kayla's vehicle near that road, so we believe she must have been trying to find it. She didn't run out of gas. As far as we can tell, there are no mechanical malfunctions. Maybe someone flagged her down. Maybe someone stopped on the pretense of giving her directions and then grabbed her. Maybe she got tired of looking and decided to go smoke a joint by the river." There's some nervous laughter. Thayer looks disappointed. Like we should have straightened up and put on horrified faces at the very idea.

And me? I wonder who told. Was it Gabie? I cut my eyes sideways at her. She's looking straight ahead. But her knees are still jiggling away.

I think of Kayla and me that one time in the cooler, and Gabie outside, ready to wait on the customers that weren't coming in. In the cooler, there's only one bulb overhead, so it's dark in the corners. We stood between crates of cheese and pepperoni and passed the joint back and forth. When I took it back from Kayla, it was wet with her spit. My lips and even my tongue were touching something she had just touched. I wanted to kiss her in the worst way. But I didn't. She was still with Brock then, and he went out for practically every sport. Even though he always looks half asleep, he's all muscle. He probably has fifty pounds on me. So Kayla and I just leaned against the cold cement wall, our shoulders touching.

I realize the cop is looking straight at me. Like he

wants me to break down and say there's a big drug ring at our school. Which is so stupid. Someone took Kayla because they wanted a girl, not because they wanted drugs. Kayla might have had a joint or two in her purse. Maybe. But no more than that, and they didn't take her purse anyway. She doesn't sell anything, and as far as I can tell, she doesn't buy, either. People just give her weed. Like I did that one time.

Thayer finally breaks the long silence. "We need to look at every possibility. At this stage of the game, we can't afford to overlook anything." He scans the room. With his sharp, long nose, he looks like the hawks that circle over the freeway looking for roadkill. "There have been reports that a white pickup was seen in the vicinity that night, so we're talking to owners of white trucks."

White truck? I'd bet every tenth car in Portland is a white pickup truck. Good luck with that one.

"Excuse me," Amber says. She only works weekends. "I heard he asked for the girl in the Mini Cooper. Doesn't that mean he really wanted Gabie?" She looks over her shoulder at Gabie and whispers "Sorry!" as if she has revealed a secret. And it's clear that for some people in the room, this is the first they are hearing about this.

Gabie freezes. At least the top part of her body does. Even her knees still for a minute.

The cop says, "We're looking at every possibility, but we think it's more than likely that this guy targeted Kayla Cutler. He may have said something about Gabriella's Mini Cooper to throw us off the scent, but he still took Kayla. Whatever happened, Kayla pulled her car to the side of the road, put it in park, set the emergency brake, and left her purse on the seat. These are the actions of a young woman who feels comfortable with her surroundings. We believe whoever was with her that night was someone she knew, or at least a familiar face. It might have been a friend, someone she knows from school, or a regular customer who is acquainted with the young women who work here."

Girls suck in their breath. Amber's eyes get wide, like she's about to cry. She pretty much only works delivery.

"That's why we need your help," the cop says. "While we've already talked to most of you, in the next few days we're going to interview everyone again. We're especially interested in hearing about any delivery customer—or any customer at all—who has made you nervous. At this point, we want to know everything, even your gut feelings."

"How are you going to keep us safe?" an older woman named Sunny demands. She works days, and mostly right here in this dough room. It's hard to imagine she's in danger; she waddles.

Pete clears his throat. "I'm changing the schedule. No more girls doing deliveries. It's going to be guys only. Guys with cars, it goes without saying."

Crap! What's that mean for me? All I have is a longboard.

"Here are the new schedules." Pete hands a stack of papers to people in the front row. They pass them back as the meeting begins to break up. When one comes to me, I see how bad it is. Lately, I've been working four days a week (and filling in whenever)—and now it's down to two.

Gabie moves her finger down to my name. "Wow— they really cut your hours."

"Yeah, it's going to suck," I say. Which is an understatement. A lot of the other kids work at Pete's for spending money or maybe to add to a college fund. For me, my hours mean food on the table and lights that come on when I flip the switch.

Before, I worked on Tuesdays and Wednesdays with Gabie. Kayla and I worked together Friday nights. And pretty much everybody worked Saturdays. But now I'm only scheduled on Fridays and Saturdays. And the two weekdays I normally work with a girl who does deliveries have been given to Miguel. I look over at him. He's still staring down at the schedule. He's a senior, too, but he's always looked older than any of us. He's over six feet tall, and his dark hair is buzzed right down to his scalp. His long, close-trimmed sideburns follow the angle of his jaw. Miguel's been shaving since sixth grade. He catches me looking at him, and I turn away. But not before I see his mean little smile.

Gabie looks up at me. "Do you have a driver's license?" Her eyes are an unusual color. Not green, not blue, not gray, not hazel. They're the kind that can look different depending on the day and the lighting and the color of a sweater.

I shrug. "Yeah, but what difference does that make? Pete doesn't have a car we can use for deliveries."

"You could use my car," she says, and then looks away.

I can't believe it. Gabie and me, we get along fine, but it's not like we're good friends. I don't even know why she works. She doesn't need to. Her parents have money—they're both doctors. Surgeons, I think. Her black Mini Cooper is probably only six months old.

Most of the rich kids at our school are popular, too. But Gabie's not in that group. She's not part of any group, really. She's quiet, always holding back, always watching.

Kind of like me.

"No," I say, but it comes out too hard. She flinches. Mentally, I curse myself. "I mean, sorry, but no thanks."

She straightens up so we're almost eye to eye. "I'm serious." She looks around until she spots Miguel. He's in the front, talking to Thayer. She turns back, and her voice gets lower. "I would much rather work with you. When I work with Miguel, all he does is slack off. Plus, he's always making vulture pies." Vulture pies are pizzas so bad they're suitable only for vultures or employees. "And then at the end of the day he takes them home. I've seen him do that with as many as three pizzas."

"I'm surprised Pete hasn't figured that out yet." Pete's incredibly cheap. Once Danny found some glass in a five-pound can of mushrooms. Instead of telling him to throw them out, Pete offered him a dollar for every piece of glass he found. Danny ended up with fourteen bucks and a big cut on his thumb.

Gabie shrugs. "Pete's been taking inventory more often, so he might be catching on. So please? Please use my car and save me from Miguel?"

I hesitate. The truth is, I need the money. Sometimes I even think about doing a fake pizza order myself. Even though by now I'm totally sick of pizza. Pete already lets us make a personal pizza for our breaks if we work more than four hours. Lately, I've been putting anchovies on mine or leaving off the cheese and putting on twice as much sauce. Anything so it doesn't taste like the thousand pizzas I've eaten before.

Gabie takes a deep breath. Then she says in a rush, "Besides, I like working with you."

I'm so surprised that for a moment I don't say anything. When we work together, she has a cautious way of looking at me. Like she thinks I might be dangerous. If I make a joke, she waits a second before she laughs. It always makes me wonder if she *is* going to laugh.

And then when she does, low and throaty, it's the kind of laugh you want to hear again.

"Would that really be cool with your insurance?"

"I could check and see." Gabie shrugs. "Besides, if you didn't get into an accident, it wouldn't matter. Nobody would know. And I'll bet you're a careful driver."

Is Gabie Klug flirting with me? With me, Drew Lyle?

"You've never seen me drive. How do you know I'm careful?"

"I can tell." She looks up at me through her lashes.

I can't believe it. She *is* flirting. "Why would you do that for me?"

And then she's suddenly serious. "Because I've seen enough to know you deserve it."

THE FOURTH DAY

GABIE

DREW AND I have to wait to talk to Pete. Amber is talking to him, or more *at* him, waving her hands.

Finally it's our turn. "Can we talk to you about the schedule?" I ask.

"Both of you?" Pete looks at me, then Drew, then back at me.

"Yes," I say firmly.

"Come into my office."

Office is kind of an overstatement for a space that's ten feet by ten. The desk is covered with receipts and a printing calculator. Boxes of pineapple and olives are stacked next to the walls. Since there's only one chair and Pete sits in it, Drew and I lean against the boxes.

I take a deep breath. "I think you should give Drew back the days you cut."

Pete shrugs. "Sorry, but he doesn't have a car. And I'm not letting you or any girl make deliveries." He pinches the bridge of his nose. "Not after what happened to Kayla."

"He can use my car."

Pete looks as surprised by this news as Drew did a few minutes ago.

"I don't know. . . ."

"Come on," I say. "I don't want to work with Miguel."

"Why not?'

"Because I wouldn't feel safe with him. If any bad guy came into the restaurant, *I* would have to be the one to protect Miguel."

It's true, too. Miguel may look like an adult, but when Danny cut his thumb, Miguel almost passed out. And if it was a choice between protecting me and running away, Miguel would run so fast his shoes would smoke.

Pete puts his hand up to his mouth, but not before I see the smile underneath his big black mustache.

"Well, I can't afford to have you decide you don't want to work here, too. Amber just told me she's not coming back." He looks at Drew. "So obviously that schedule I passed out is already out the window. Would you be interested in extra hours?"

"Sure." Drew never says no to extra hours.

"I appreciate you guys sticking it out. I can see how it might affect you. Both of you," Pete says. His eyes, which turn down at the corners, make him look like a sad hound dog.

"That's all I think about," Drew says softly. I don't say anything, just nod.

Pete leans closer. "I'll tell you guys something, but you can't tell anyone."

"Okay," we both say. Drew shoots a glance at me, and I can tell he feels like I do. Like maybe he doesn't really want to know.

"They found a spot down by the river, not far from Kayla's car. A place where the river bank was all torn up. Like there was a struggle. They also found a rock about the size of a fist with blood on it. They're running tests on it now. They're getting DNA from Kayla's toothbrush or something to see if it matches. But if it *is* blood, it's probably hers."

"A rock?" Drew echoes. "Next to the river?"

Pete nods. I don't know about them, but I'm thinking about the river, how deep and wide and fast it is. Parts are over a hundred feet deep. The spring snowmelt has been high this year.

Pete adds quickly, "But don't tell anyone. It could be a coincidence."

"Do her parents know?" Drew asks.

"Of course," Pete says, already looking like he's sorry that he told us. "But no one else. I really shouldn't have said anything." He busies himself straightening up some papers. It's clear we're being dismissed. "I'll talk to Miguel and tell him the schedule's changed back."

Outside Pete's office, I turn to Drew. "Want to go to Starbucks?"

DREW'S MOM came into Pete's a couple of weeks ago. Drew was in the back, grating mozzarella on the Hobart. I didn't know it was his mom. He and I went to different elementary schools, which is about the last time you see people's parents.

My first thought wasn't that she was anyone's mom. Her dishwater blond hair hung in tangled curls in front of her skinny face, and her blue eyeshadow was smeared over one eye. She had on jeans, a black down jacket, and scuffed high heels.

"Hey, is Drew working today?" She had a smoker's voice, and she smelled like one too.

"He's in the back," I said. "Do you want me to get him for you?"

Everyone at school knew you could buy weed off Drew Lyle. But it was all pretty casual, a couple of joints. It wasn't like he was some big dealer. He only sold pot. But now it looked like he was selling it to adults as well as kids, and somehow that was different. Plus, I'd never seen him sell at work before. I didn't like that idea at all.

Instead of answering me, she suddenly bellowed, "Drew! Come out here! Drew!"

I winced. There was only one other customer in the place, some guy in his thirties who was eating a slice at the counter and reading an old *People* magazine. He had tried to hit on me earlier. I pegged him for recently divorced. And probably for good reason. I had communicated with him as little as possible, and he had given up, his shoulders slumping. Maybe he had finally realized how ridiculous he was being, trying to flirt with a seventeen-year-old girl at a pizza place. Now he looked up with an expression of annoyance that quickly changed to one of contemplation. Fresh meat. Or not so fresh.

She opened her mouth to yell again. "I'll get him," I said quickly, not wanting to hear another nasal bray.

But Drew came out at a run.

"Mom, what are you doing here?"

Mom? She didn't look any older than thirty.

And the look Drew shot me couldn't be characterized. Embarrassed, defiant, pleading.

"I need," Drew's mom announced in a haughty voice, "to borrow some money."

THE FOURTH DAY

DREW

AT STARBUCKS, Gabie insists on paying. I wish I'd ordered a house coffee instead of a grande mocha.

"Are you guys related?" the barista says as she hands over identical coffees.

We laugh, say no, and then look at each other. We do kind of look alike. I'm two inches taller, but we both have straight chin-length hair that's the same nothing color, not blond, not brown, with bangs some people might think are too long.

"Thanks for the coffee, cuz." I lift the cup toward Gabie, like I'm making a toast. She smiles. We go out and sit at one of the small round metal tables. The sun feels good, like a warm, flat hand on my back.

The only other person outside is a guy smoking and talking on a cell phone. Still, Gabie lowers her voice. "One of the reasons I wanted to talk to you is I feel like you're the only one who understands about Kayla. I mean, he wanted me, right? He asked for the girl in the Mini Cooper. He didn't ask for Kayla. She was an innocent bystander."

"He did ask about you."

Gabie's throat moves up and down as she swallows. She's quiet for a long time, but then she says in a rush, "Sometimes I think—what if he still wants me? What if he comes back?" Her knees are going again. I want to put my palm on them, like you would try to soothe a frightened animal.

"Well, you won't be making deliveries anymore," I point out. "But if you feel scared, you could just quit."

Her mouth twists. "What good would that do? If he wants me, he can get me whether I'm at Pete's or not. In fact, it's probably better that I'm at work, because at least there are other people around."

"What about your parents?"

"They're hardly ever home. They do a lot of trauma surgery, which means they're on call twenty-four hours." She picks at the lip of her paper cup, uncurling a tiny section. "I'll wake up in the morning and realize I'm the only one in the house and have been all night. It's spooky, even if the alarm is on."

I nod. It's not the same, but sometimes my mom goes home with some guy she's met. Still, the end result is the same: you wake up in an empty house.

"Have you talked to the police? Maybe they could get you a bodyguard."

"Oh, right." She rolls her eyes. "They seem to think it was someone who knew Kayla. You heard them today. They think the reason she got out of the car was because she knew the person. But he asked for *me*." Gabie stabs her chest with her index finger. She's wearing some kind of white gauzy blouse with a pink tank top underneath.

"Maybe he asked for you to throw the cops off the scent like Thayer said. Maybe whoever it was already knew Kayla was working that night."

I don't really believe it, but Gabie looks a tiny bit relieved.

"Then who would it be?" Her eyes narrow. "Do you think it could be Brock? Kayla just broke up with him. Isn't that when there's the most danger for violence?"

I try to imagine Brock angry, angry enough to hurt or kill Kayla. Underneath his half-closed eyes and barely passing grades, maybe there's a coil of energy and rage, just waiting to spring out.

But I don't think so.

"He could just wait until after school or go over to Kayla's house on a weekend or something," I point out. "Why go to all the trouble of calling in a fake pizza order?"

"The same reason anyone would do it," Gabie says darkly. "So they would have privacy, out there in the middle of nowhere. So they could do whatever they wanted to her with no witnesses." She stands up, chugs the rest of her mocha in a single gulp, and tosses it in the garbage can. "Will you go somewhere with me?"

I've worked with Gabie for fourteen months, but today I've said more to her than in all those months put together. Plus she keeps surprising me.

"Sure. Where?"

"I want to see."

"What?" I think I know what she's saying, but I'm hoping I'm wrong.

"I want to see the place for myself. Where it happened. Will you come with me?"

"Okay," I say and push back my chair. A snake uncoils in my belly. Is this really a good idea? I wonder if we'll even be able to find where it happened. At Pete's we have a big map of the area we can check before we go out on an order.

I have a sudden flash of Kayla looking at it before she left, tracing her finger on a line running parallel to the river. And then she turned and said something to me, didn't she?

But I still can't remember what.

I've never been in a Mini Cooper before. It's cool. The dash is wood and shaped like a *T*, with a speedometer as big as a plate. Instead of an annoying *beep, beep, beep* to remind you about the seat belt, it plays a three-note melody that sounds straight from the disco era. It almost makes me smile.

As I get into the passenger seat, Gabie hands me some papers. It's MapQuest directions to the fake address.

"How did you get it to give you directions?" I ask. "I thought the cops said this address didn't exist."

"I guess MapQuest doesn't know that. It must just figure out where the address *should* be and give directions to that spot. Even if it's not real."

Despite the directions, the address is hard to find. Once we get off the main road, we don't pass a single car. The roads are narrow, barely big enough for two cars to pass, with gravel shoulders. There's no houses out here, no nothing. Just a sign, pockmarked with bullet holes, warning there's a five-hundred-dollar fine for dumping trash. The road where the house supposedly was is next to what the Internet says is a Superfund site. Fifty years ago, companies dumped tar and creosote into the river before conveniently going bankrupt so they wouldn't have to pay for any cleanup.

I see something white in the distance, but it takes a while to recognize it. Someone has put up a white cross next to the road, the way people do to mark where someone died in a car accident. We park about twenty feet away. After getting out of the car, we walk toward it without saying anything. Our feet crunch on the gravel. The river rushes on our right, but I can't see it.

Looking at the cross is creepy. Crosses mean dead people, but no one has said Kayla's dead. Maybe Kayla's parents already know more than Pete, know that it is her blood, or have even already identified her body. I imagine her being pulled from the water, her skin so white it's nearly violet, her tangled black hair covering her face.

Kayla's senior picture is glued to the center where the two wooden sticks meet. One arm of the cross says KAYLA in purple glitter. The other arm says CUTLER. A purple teddy bear is propped at the base.

"When I think of Kayla, I don't think of white crosses or purple teddy bears," I tell Gabie. Kayla never talked about religion, and she doesn't seem like the kind of girl who still likes stuffed animals.

"You never know." Gabie takes a deep breath and her lips tremble. "Chase me."

I hear what she says, but I can't understand it. Or I understand it all right, but I can't believe it. "What?"

"Chase me. Chase me down to the river."

I stop pretending I don't know what she means. "It's

58

still light out," I point out. "It was dark then. It's not the same."

"Please," she urges, "chase me." She runs a few steps, stops. Her eyes are shiny.

"That's crazy. That's sick. You heard the cop. He wanted Kayla."

Gabie shakes her head so hard her hair whips out. "I don't think so." Her face wrinkles up. She presses her fingers against her lips. She looks like she's going to cry or throw up. "It was supposed to be me," she whispers from behind her fingers.

I puff air out of my lips. "But why do you want me to chase you?"

"I'm freaking out, Drew! I can't stop thinking about it. I need to know what it was like for Kayla."

THE FOURTH DAY

GABIE

I IMAGINE KAYLA running. I've seen her run the bases before. She's fast. Tricky. She takes chances, takes a lead off the base, daring the pitcher to pick her off. She steals when she can. Always with a grin.

In my mind's eye, Kayla's running into the dark, her hands in front of her, her breath coming in panicked gasps.

But why did she get out of the car? She could have locked the doors or leaned on the horn; she could have used her cell phone or driven away. She could have run him over. I imagine her punching the gas, the satisfying *thunk* as he disappeared under her bumper.

But instead Kayla got out of the car. And then she must have run. For whatever reason, she didn't get back in. Maybe he was between her and the car. Or did she try, did Kayla try to stay in the car, and he dragged her out while she kicked and screamed? But then I remember how they found her purse, still sitting on the passenger seat, undisturbed. So whatever happened happened outside the car.

Kayla set the parking brake. She got out of the car. Was she by herself then? But if she was by herself, why would she get the pizzas? There's no house nearby. She would only do that if she thought she was with whoever had ordered them.

Or did the guy grab them after he had done whatever he did to her, come back to her car, his job finished, and take them? Only then he panicked, maybe at the sound of a car, and dropped them and ran away.

My thoughts go back to Kayla, running from the car. It's all I can think about.

And that's when I start to run. In a second, I hear Drew's footsteps behind me. He's calling, "Gabie, stop this! Gabie!"

I cut down the slope, heading for the sound of the river. It's hidden by a line of bushes and trees.

Did she scream, her voice echoing through the empty night? Or did she save her breath so she could run faster? Did Kayla try to keep her footsteps light, so he couldn't follow her in the dark? With the river so close, the sound of the water might have given her some cover. I imagine her running, her hands outstretched in front of her, thinking, thinking—which way could she go? Where could she be safe? Was there any place she could hide?

And all the time she's running as fast as she can. Running from the man hunting her.

I close my eyes, imagining the blackness that night, but my lids flutter open a second later.

He must have caught her. Why else was there a bloody rock down by the river?

Drew's fingertips graze my shoulder, and just like that, my adrenaline pumps even harder. My breath is coming in gasps. Drew's staying right on my heels.

How did the guy catch Kayla? Did he grab her shoulder? Or was she wearing her hair in a ponytail that night? Did he snatch it, jerking her head back? I see her crying out, falling to her knees, sharp rocks cutting her hands. Maybe that's where the blood came from.

And here it is, the river, dark gray and about fifty feet across. A ten-foot slope covered with weeds and stunted bushes leads down to it, and then there's the bank itself, edged with lots of broken black rocks. Nobody would walk along here if they could help it. The dirt closest to the river looks stained and oily. About a hundred feet farther down, one area's all churned up. No yellow crime scene tape, but I don't need any to know this is where they found the bloody rock. I realize I've stopped running, stopped moving altogether.

Drew catches up with me, swearing under his breath. Together, we walk over to the spot that stands out because of what isn't there. It's like Kayla herself. Her absence sets off echoes. At work, I keep expecting to hear her voice or see her laughing at the counter.

I look down at the broken ground. Was this the last place where Kayla drew a breath, made a sound?

But I still can't believe it. I just can't.

What if there were two of them? That's an even worse thought. Two men, not one. What kind of a chance would Kayla have had then? None at all. One could hold her while the other one did whatever he wanted to her— slapped her, tore off her clothes. Or hit her with a rock.

And why the rock? Did she cut her hand falling? Or was it something worse? Had the bad things happened yet, or was it just the beginning? Or—and my heart quickens here—maybe Kayla was the one who hefted the rock. Maybe she hit him in the head and then fled the quickest way she could, by jumping into the river. But how could she survive a nighttime swim in swift-moving water?

And that's when I kick off my shoes. I barely register Drew yelling, "What the hell are you doing?" I hold my breath and leap.

The water is an icy shock. You hear about spring snowmelt, but all that's an abstraction until you're in it. For a second, I can't breathe, I can't think, I can't figure out what to do with my arms and legs.

And then it comes back to me. I take a deep breath and start treading water. Still, every eggbeater kick is an effort. My arms are leaden, my legs numb.

I'm a good swimmer. When I was fourteen, I was a junior lifeguard, but Drew doesn't know that. All he knows is I'm in the water. He stares at me from shore, his face open and frightened.

I'm about to call to him, to tell him I'm okay, when suddenly he kicks off his own shoes and throws himself into the water. I realize he's trying to save me.

But it's pretty clear Drew is not much of a swimmer. And the current is carrying both of us downstream.

His head sinks lower, low enough that water goes over his lips. And Drew reacts like someone who's just stuck his finger in a light socket. He's rigid and fighting, all at once.

Then his head goes completely under and he comes

up gasping, hyperventilating, just plain freaking out. Little spots of sunshine are dancing on the water, and I realize Drew might die right here, right now. And it will be my fault.

All I really want to do is curl up in a ball. I'm still so cold. Instead, I swim toward Drew. He keeps sputtering, lifting his head out of the water, looking for me. From my lifeguard training, I remember to approach him from behind, so he can't climb on top of me in a panic and take me underwater. Only since he can't see me, he is panicking even more.

Once I get close to him, I yell, "Don't grab on to me!"

He manages to spin around, his expression a weird mixture of fear and relief.

Then he goes underwater for the second time.

I snag the back of his shirt and start pulling him in.

By the time I reach the bank, my body is done. We lie next to each other, half in and half out of the water, panting. I want to pull myself completely onto the bank, but I can't summon the energy.

Drew levers himself up on his elbow. "What the hell were you trying to do?" he croaks out, but with each word his voice strengthens. "You almost killed me. Do you realize that? You almost killed me!"

He shakes my shoulder, and then his hand slips and he's on top of me. I'm crying and trying to hit him.

He grabs my wrists and pins me down. I arch my back and try to buck him off. The old-penny taste of blood floods my mouth.

His face contorts with fear and anger. "Are you crazy?"

I start to sob, huge sobs that must have been stored up in my chest for the past three days.

"Maybe I am. It was supposed to be me," I choke out. "It was supposed to be me."

With a groan, Drew throws himself down on the rocks beside me. He looks different with his hair plastered to his skull. More vulnerable.

"Maybe it was," he says quietly, "but that's not how it worked out. It's not up to you to kill yourself to prove they made a mistake. Kayla wouldn't want that."

My sobs slow down, get spaced further apart, and finally stop.

"You know what the strangest thing is?" I whisper. "I feel like she's alive. I'm not talking about her spirit. I'm talking about the real Kayla. It feels like she's alive."

THE FOURTH DAY

DREW

GABIE IS CLEARLY a mess. Trying to kill herself, trying to kill me.

I don't know what to do or say. And then I start to laugh.

She levers herself up on one elbow. "Why are you laughing?" Her eyes are narrowed. But one corner of her mouth crooks up like she wants to be let in on the joke. Her hair is tangled.

"Because I've worked with you for what—more than a year?—and I would never have guessed in a million years you would act like that. Aren't you supposed to be the responsible one?"

Her head snaps back like I slapped her. "What's that supposed to mean?"

"Hey, don't act all insulted. Everyone knows that your parents are these big-shot doctors. And that you're always on the honor roll. I've seen you work, remember? You follow all of Pete's rules. You weigh everything. You always use the pusher on the Hobart. You won't let me turn the closed sign over even two minutes early. You're the good girl."

"That's just it." Gabie heaves a shaky sigh. "I feel responsible. If Kayla hadn't asked to trade with me, it would have been me in that car. Not her." She turns to look at the water, lapping only inches from us. Her voice is so soft I have to strain to hear. "Me being thrown in the river."

"She's the one who asked to trade, not you," I point out. Still, I know all about guilt. I know all about feeling like you should have been able to stop something.

But why did Gabie have to dive in the river? Even though we're on the riverbank, the sun already drying out our clothes, part of me still feels like I'm thrashing in the water. Feeling it close over my head, my feet searching for the bottom and not finding it. Water burning my nose and throat. My lungs all hollow with need.

In that same faded voice, Gabie says, "In some ways, it makes more sense that someone took Kayla."

"What do you mean?"

"Because she's pretty. Prettier than me."

I sit all the way up. "That's just whack. Are you saying girls who are pretty deserve to be kidnapped? They deserve whatever happens to them?"

"No," she says.

But I'm not sure she means it.

TRANSCRIPT OF 911 CALL

911 Operator: Police, fire, or medical?

Unknown male caller: Police.

911 Operator: What is the nature of your emergency?

Unknown male caller: It's about that missing girl. Kayla Cutler. Ask Cody Renfrew about it. Ask him. Ask him why he painted his truck. Because it was white, and that's the color they said on the news. The color of the truck that took that girl. Cody's truck used to be white. Now all of a sudden, it's brown. Ask him where he was Wednesday night. Ask him.

THE FOURTH DAY

GABIE

I'M SITTING in front of my computer. It's nearly midnight, but my parents are at the hospital. There was some five-car pileup on I-5, Jaws of Life, Life Flight, etc., the kind of thing that means their weekend just became a work-day. I'm eating one of three snack-sized bags of Ruffles Sour Cream and Cheddar chips I bought at Subway after work. I'm too scared to buy a big bag at Safeway when it's dark, even if I park right up front.

I've decided this day has been weird enough that I deserve to eat junk food. Even though normally the housekeeper who comes in twice a week empties the gar-bage, I'll take the empty bags to school Monday so my mom doesn't see them and lecture me about cholesterol, sodium, and trans fats.

My head is all jumbled up with what happened today. Seeing Sergeant Thayer again. Pete telling us about the bloody rock. Offering Drew my car without even think-ing about it. Driving to the river and everything that hap-pened there. Drew and I went back to work, and I tried to pretend I hadn't told him the things I had been thinking.

Tried to act around him the way I act around everyone. Like we hadn't gone down to the river, hadn't seen that white cross, hadn't nearly drowned. Hadn't rolled over each other on the riverbank.

Right now, I'm not even tasting the chips, just cramming them in my mouth while I look online. It's scary how many sites there are for missing people. Most of them are crowded with too many words, too many fonts, too many pixilated clip-art pictures of roses and angels and candles. Some of them are sad remnants left up even though the person they were created to find isn't missing anymore. At the top of one Web page is a newspaper story headlined "Prep School Student Admits Killing Girl with Bat."

I click and click, until I end up at missingkids.com. It's like a clearinghouse for kids all over the United States who have disappeared. You can search by name, by sex, by year, by state.

I just type in Oregon and hit return. There are nearly fifty kids who have gone missing in Oregon over the last twenty years. I click on the listings one by one. The recent listings have only a single photo that shows a chubby toddler or a sullen-looking teen. The ones who disappeared a long time ago have two photos, a dated-looking picture from when they first went missing and a second updated by a computer program, so you can see what they should have looked like when they turned thirty or forty or even older.

Sucking orange cheese dust from my fingers, I'm looking at an entry for a guy who was twelve when he disappeared in 1987. He has a photo labeled "Age Progression." I have a feeling this stocky man in a blue polo shirt with a shaving nick on his Adam's apple never existed outside of Photoshop. That he was only bones well before he had a chance to be an adult.

I click and click, until the details blur together. They went to the mall, to the fair, to church—only they never came home. Sometimes they never went anyplace but to bed. They were last seen with friends, with three boys, on the beach with an older man, getting into a car, going fishing, getting off the bus. They have gaps between their teeth, freckles, a mole on their nose, need medication. They grin at me from school portraits or family photos.

Underneath their photos are sad scraps of facts. "Tyler's photo is shown age-progressed to 24 years. He was last seen in his bed. He has warts on his right foot." Tyler has been missing for twenty-one years. Those warts must be long gone, one way or another.

I don't realize that I'm crying until a hot tear plops on my thigh.

CITY OF ROSES LAB REPORT

DNA from a toothbrush belonging to Kayla Cutler (Exhibit A) as well as from blood on a rock found by the Willamette River (Exhibit B) was amplified using the Polymerase Chain Reaction (PCR) and profiled at the loci listed on the attached table.

A single human DNA profile was identified in Exhibit B which matches the DNA profile of Kayla Cutler obtained from Exhibit A. This profile would be expected to occur in approximately 1 in 273 billion unrelated individuals.

The evidence will be held in the laboratory vault and may be picked up at your earliest convenience.

FROM THE WEB SITE OF TREVOR G. SMITH, CRIMINAL DEFENSE ATTORNEY

Q: Why should I never talk to the police or law enforcement agencies about a crime?

A: Regardless of whether you think you are guilty or innocent of a crime, you should never talk to the police before you first talk with an attorney. The police often lead people to believe they will receive a lesser penalty if they confess. Usually, the opposite is true. After you have an attorney and negotiate an agreement, then you may benefit from giving information to the police.

Q: Can the police lie to me?

A: Yes! Many people are surprised that the police are allowed to lie. Think about it; they lie every day when they pretend to be drug buyers and instead are undercover narcotics detectives. Or they pretend to be johns and tell prostitutes that they are customers. The sad truth is the American justice system allows police officers to lie. And they will lie if they think it will build a case against you.

The United States Supreme Court has ruled that the police can lie to you in order to extract a confession. Police officers are also allowed to lie about evidence. For example, in a 1978 case, the police said they had compared the defendant's fingerprints to a fingerprint on the victim's checkbook and that they matched. Actually, no fingerprints were found on the checkbook. The defendant then confessed to the robbery. The Court later ruled that the police deception did not invalidate a voluntary confession.

TRANSCRIPT OF POLICE INTERVIEW
WITH CODY RENFREW

Today's date is May 11, and it is approximately 10:30 A.M. Myself—
Sergeant R. F. Thayer with the Portland Police Department—and
FBI Special Agent Berkeley Moore as well as Cody Renfrew are
present. At this time, I am going to advise you of your rights. You
have the right to remain silent. Anything you say can and will be
used against you in a court of law. You have the right to speak
with an attorney and have him or her present with you while you
are being questioned. If you cannot afford an attorney, one will be
appointed to represent you before any questioning if you wish. You
can decide at any time to exercise these rights and not answer
any questions or make any statements. Do you understand these
rights, which I have explained to you?

R: Yeah.

T: Could you speak up for me?

R: Yeah.

T: Okay, having these rights in mind, are you willing to speak with
us and allow us to talk with you?

R: I'll listen, yeah, I'll listen to you.

T: Are you willing to sign this?

R: So what is this—I sign over my rights?

T: All it is is you are basically saying we told you these rights and you understand them and you're willing to talk to us. You're not signing any rights away. If you don't want to talk with us, don't talk with us. If you want to stop, you can stop.

R: Okay, yeah, I'll sign it.

T: Sign right down on that line.

R: Okay.

T: We're here to talk to you today about this girl, Kayla Cutler, who you know.

R: I don't know her. You can't pin this on me.

T: But you went to school with Kayla. You were in the same grade as her older brother, Kyle.

R: Dude, I barely knew Kyle. I haven't seen him since graduation. Kayla's three years younger than me, so I really didn't know her.

T: When was the last time you saw her?

R: I don't know. In high school, I guess. Three years ago. She would have been a freshman when I was a senior. But I'm telling you, I don't know her.

T: Look, Cody, I am sure there is a reason that what happened happened. Whether this girl came at you for no reason, maybe confronted you, or she had a weapon, tried to fight with you, something of that nature. I don't know what the reason was. But that's why we're here. There are always two sides to every story. And anything you say could be mitigating circumstances for you. I just want to get your side.

R: But I don't have a side. I didn't have nothing to do with this. Look, I feel really bad for her and everything, but I didn't do anything to her.

T: Cody, Cody, Cody. It is not a matter of whether you did or didn't do it. Because I've got your blood on the rock you used to bash her head. DNA doesn't lie.

R: But it has to be a lie. There's no way.

T: I have the lab report sitting right on my desk.

R: That's just messed up. Someone must have made a mistake. Like at the lab. Because I didn't pick up no rock. I'm telling you, I don't even know this girl.

T: You wouldn't be here right now if it weren't for the evidence. And we've got a seventeen-year-old girl we can't find. There are so many questions I would like the answers to. And I think it would be nice to get that off your shoulders, because I'm sure it's probably been bothering you. Maybe she argued with you. That wouldn't surprise me, the things I've heard about her.

M: What happened more than likely was an accident. I'm sure you didn't go out with the intent to kill anybody. Did she come at you, and you had to fight her off and then she accidentally fell into the river? Is that what happened? Right now I think it would help the family tremendously if they knew what happened to their daughter. I think they have a right to know what went down. I mean, it wouldn't surprise me one bit if she turned on you. That wouldn't surprise me one bit.

T: That girl was known to have a temper. Some people say she's real mean. But the bottom line is that if you don't get that out there, if you don't get that story told, it's going to look bad.

R: I want to get something straight. I didn't kill anybody. I didn't murder anybody. I never saw Kayla until I saw her on TV, and I never touched a single hair on her head.

T: Okay, then who did?

R: I don't know, dude. How am I supposed to know?

M: Why did you paint your truck?

R: It got a scratch on it.

T: A scratch? You just happened to get a scratch on it, and you just happened to think to paint it the day that it comes out that we're looking for a white truck in connection with Kayla Cutler's disappearance?

R: Maybe I heard about that. Maybe I heard about it and didn't want no one looking in the wrong direction.

M: But you were down by the river, Cody. You were there. We have an eyewitness who saw your truck near where that girl's car was found.

R: I might have been near there, maybe, but I never saw that girl.

T: Okay. Well, let's talk about what you were doing down by the river.

R: Uh.

T: What were you doing out there? I mean out of all the places to be, you just happen to be at a place where a girl goes missing.

R: Shoot, it happens.

M: Yeah, but you don't live anywhere close. What were you doing out there?

R: Okay. Here's the thing. I'm only telling you this because I ain't got nothing to do with that girl, that Kayla chick.

T: What were you doing?

R: Sometimes I sell scrap metal. There was some down there. It's just scrap. It don't belong to anybody.

T: Look, we're not interested if you're stealing metal and selling it. We're only interested in where Kayla is. If you help us with that, we can make everything else go away.

M: You know, Cody, how sometimes things happen like in a dream, only they're real, but they feel like a dream? I know I've had that happen to me. It's like you're sleepwalking and you don't even really know what happened. It's not like you decide to do something, it's more like it just happens all by itself. Is that what happened with this girl? Something happened that wasn't your fault?

R: It's not like that, man. It's not like that.

M: Then tell us what it is like. That's why we're here.

R: Okay, look. I seen another car that night, man. And there was a dude driving it. He was there. You should be looking for him.

T: What kind of car?

R: I don't know, man.

T: I mean big car, little car, red, green, white—what kind of car?

R: Silver? Maybe silver. And average size. But it's not like I knew something bad was going to happen that night and you were going to be asking me all these questions. I saw a car drive by. And there was a guy in it.

T: How old was he? What did he look like?

R: I don't know. Maybe as old as my dad. And his hair looked dark. I only saw him for a second.

T: But if you were there, then I'm sure you actually know who this guy is. And then it comes off of you. Because if you aren't the one that did it, then someone else did.

M: I think someone was with you, Cody, and they're the one who really did it. The flip side is, the longer you wait, the more chance that somebody else is going to tell their side of a story that doesn't sound good for you. And then you won't ever get to tell your side because then we won't need to talk to you. Your story won't get told.

R: But I don't have a story.

M: Were you taking that scrap metal where you saw the girl? She was lost, and she asked you for directions and then what happened? She got pissy with you, is that it? She saw what you were doing, and she called you on it.

R: What? I never saw no girl. I saw another car, I already told you that. But I never saw that girl, and I never touched a hair on her head. I've told you everything I know.

T: But—

R: I've told you everything I know. You said I could say stop when I wanted. Well, stop. I say stop. I don't want to talk to you anymore.

M: Okay, okay.

T: Maybe not us. But I want you to think about talking to someone else.

R: I already told you, I'm done talking. I don't want to talk to the police.

T: She's not the police. Her name is Elizabeth Lamb. She's a psychic. The family hired her to find out what happened to Kayla. They need to know. She might be able to help you remember.

R: I don't know. I might. Maybe. But with no recorder. And no people behind mirrors. Just me and her. That's it.

THE SIXTH DAY

GABIE

I TAKE A DEEP breath before I push open the main door to school on Monday morning. Is it my imagination, or are people staring at me? But then I catch part of a whisper, and I know I'm not imagining it. Because this black-haired girl whose name I don't know is looking right at me and whispering Kayla's name.

A knowing nod from the girl's friend, Jade. I've known Jade since third grade, but now she stares at me like I'm not really a person. I'm like a human TV program, maybe *True Crime Stories* crossed with *America's Most Wanted*.

Even those kids who have never watched TV news or picked up a newspaper know what's going on. Chase Skloot comes up to me as I'm walking to my first class. "Is it true that you switched shifts with Kayla? That you were supposed to be working that night?"

"She asked me to trade." Everyone knows who Chase is, but he has never said one word to me in his whole life. I've seen him talking to Kayla, though.

He tilts his head to one side. "Do you feel, like, you know, it should have been you?"

That stings, but I just walk away with my head down.

Our history teacher, Mrs. Sleater, starts off class by announcing that a counselor will be available all day for anyone who wants to talk about Kayla's kidnapping.

"And murder," a guy named Jason adds.

"We don't know that, Jason," Mrs. Sleater reprimands him. "Not yet."

AT LUNCH PERIOD, I've just finished paying when someone touches my arm. It's Brock Chambers, Kayla's ex-boyfriend. "Can you talk to me for a second?"

I glance around the cafeteria. Everyone is staring at us. Everyone. Even the people I eat lunch with are watching with their mouths open.

Brock usually looks sleepy, but today he just seems sad. Looking at him, I think there's no way he would hurt Kayla. Even if she hurt him. He's got these eyelids that pretty much stay at half-mast, like he can't decide whether it would be better to be awake or asleep. Usually he doesn't say much, although he has an unhurried, spacy smile. Because he's on every team except the Mathletes, everyone knows him, so our walk over to a table in a far corner of the room is interrupted by people calling his name, or saying "hey," or nodding. A few smile, but then you see their eyes flicker, like the smile is a reflex they're embarrassed by.

He's wearing a red T-shirt that says KILLSWITCH, which I'm pretty sure is some kind of band. It's tight over his muscled arms. Brock's built like a series of squares and rectangles—square shoulders, a cube for a head, arms and legs thick as trunks.

"So, you know, I'm Brock," he says as he walks to a table at the back where two guys from the football team are sitting. "Kayla's boyfriend. Well, ex-boyfriend."

I've waited on him a dozen times, or started to, before Kayla ran squealing to the front, but he obviously doesn't remember that. All I say is, "I'm Gabie."

When we get to the table, the other two guys who were there stand up. They don't say anything. They just take their trays and leave.

I sit down. Right now, the last thing I want to do is eat my burrito with its oily side of refried beans. "Brock, I'm so sorry about Kayla." I push a forkful of beans from one side of the plate to the other.

"Thanks," he says softly. Maybe that's not the right thing to say, especially when no one knows what happened, but what is the right thing? He is staring at the floor, with its black round circles where generations of kids have spit out their gum.

Brock's first question is one I don't expect. "Did she talk about me very much?" His eyes are all the way open now, and they plead with me.

I look away. "Kayla and I, it's not like we were really friends. You should be asking her real friends, not me. We just worked together."

He looks down at his hands, which are as big as catcher's mitts. "She was just always so happy. I don't know anyone else like her, always smiling. She never got mad, she was never depressed. She was just"—he runs his flat hand in a straight line across the table in front of him—"even." He can't decide what tense to use.

"Why did you break up?" It's hard to believe I'm asking this question of Brock. Harder still to believe he's answering it.

"It was her idea." I wonder if I'm imagining it, but his voice sounds rough. "We'll be going to different schools in the fall. She said she knew we wouldn't be together then, so there was no use putting it off. Except I'm wondering if that was the real reason. Because she asked you to trade so she could have Friday off, right?"

I nod. It seems like everyone knows this.

"So who was she going out with on Friday? Do you know?"

What do I say? Do I say I don't know? That's true. She never said a name. Or do I tell him another truth, how Kayla's face softened and her eyes lit up? She looked like someone in love. That's true, too.

I settle for "She didn't say why she wanted to trade. Just that it was a favor."

"Do you think it was a customer? Someone at school? Did she say anything about him?"

Everyone keeps thinking I know something, but I don't. And even if I did, would it matter? Whoever wanted to take her out on Friday night probably didn't kidnap her two days before.

"She didn't say anything at all. She just said there was something she wanted to do on Friday."

"I hear the guy asked about you. Do *you* know who it was that took her?"

I stiffen. "What? Why are you asking me that? Don't you think I would have told the police if I did?"

He waves his hand. "I know, I know, sorry. It's just that—maybe there are things you would tell me that you wouldn't tell them."

"To be honest, Brock, if I was going to tell anyone anything, it would be the police. Because I want Kayla found."

He makes a small wordless sound, and again I wonder if I hear the beginnings of tears. "What will there be to find? Whoever did it is not going to just let her come walking home again." And even though it's his table, not mine, he stands up, picks up his tray of uneaten food, and says, "Thanks for talking to me," before he walks off.

On my way back to class, I pass what must be Kayla's locker. Now it's decorated with yellow ribbons. On the floor in front of it are a half dozen bouquets of flowers, still wrapped in plastic. But the flowers are already fading, their heads hanging limp from the stems.

If I disappeared, who, besides my parents, would really miss me?

THE SIXTH DAY

KAYLA

AT SOME POINT I noticed the water bottles lined up along the bottom of the bookshelf underneath the TV, and I drank some. There was a box of granola bars, too, but they are long gone. Mostly, I've just been sleeping. Maybe it's a bad thing to sleep when you have a concussion, but I do it anyway. Sometimes I scream for help, but less and less often. I try to ignore how my stomach hurts, how it spasms.

This time when I wake up, a man is standing over me. His arms are crossed.

"Help me." I reach my hand toward him, but he steps back with a frown.

I push myself up so my back is against the wall next to the bed.

He stares at me, expressionless, and doesn't make a sound. He's wearing tan pants and a navy blue short-sleeve shirt with a row of pens in the pocket. He's got thinning dark hair and little round wire-framed glasses. He looks kind of familiar, but I can't place him.

"Scream as loud as you want," he says, and smiles. The smile changes his face, makes his eyes go flat.

I don't scream. I don't even cry. Or beg. Instead I say, "Who are you? Why am I here?"

"You belong to me now." He says it as if it's a simple fact.

The collar on his shirt is buttoned up tight, but right above it are three parallel marks, like the tops of angry red furrows. I think they're scratch marks.

And I think I made them. Looking at them, I feel a surge of pride.

Pride and fear.

And a red-hot desire to hurt him again.

My eyes cut to the door, smudged with my bloody fingerprints. It's closed. But maybe it's not locked. Quickly, before I can telegraph what I'm about to do, I shoot past him with my arm outstretched. My hand closes on the knob at the same time his closes on my shoulder. He yanks me back just as I register that the door is still locked.

"You're a bad, dirty girl," he says, and throws me onto the bed.

I stand up really fast so that he doesn't get on top of me. He just narrows his eyes. He's so close I can smell his sour breath, but my back is against the wall and I can't go any farther.

Finally he says, "You shall call me master."

"What?" I heard what he said. I just can't believe it.

He lifts his chin. "From now on, you shall call me master." He watches me. Waits for my reaction. He looks like my cat after she sees a bird in the garden. Still, but all quivery.

"Say it," he urges.

But I don't say anything. When he moves, I don't even see his hand coming.

Slap!

He hits me so hard that I fall against the white wall. Stars bloom behind my eyes. My ear is ringing. On boneless legs, I slide down to the cheap-looking linoleum. It's cool against my cheek. The gold flecks twinkle. Or maybe that's happening someplace in my eyes. In my broken head.

When I push myself up, there's a new smear of rusty blood on the wall. I touch the cut gingerly. My fingers come away wet and red.

His nose wrinkles when he sees the blood. "You shall call me master," he repeats.

"You're my master," I say.

Not meeting his eyes.

THE SIXTH DAY

GABIE

WHEN THE LAST bell rings, I run down the hall to catch Drew. I find him pulling his skateboard out of his locker.

"Do you have your wallet with you?"

His eyebrows pull together, and his hand reaches toward his back pocket like he thinks someone might have stolen it. "Yeah. Why?"

I press my keys into his palm. "Good. Then you can drive me home. You need the practice."

"What? Now?"

"I just want to make sure that you're comfortable driving my car before you have to deliver your first order tomorrow."

"Okay." He looks down at the key ring, which has two house keys and the key fob for the Mini. "What is this thing?"

"It's the key."

He runs his index finger over it. "It doesn't look like any key I've ever seen." It's round, about the size of one of those dollar coins, with concave sides. It kind of looks like the starship *Enterprise*. There's nothing metal sticking out of it.

"Trust me, it's the key," I say as we walk out to the student parking lot. I see people noticing me. It reminds me of this girl, Jordan, who went to our school last year. Her older brother took their dad's gun, went downtown, and shot into a crowd waiting for a movie to start. He hit seven people, killing two, and then shot himself in the head. Before her brother did that, no one noticed Jordan. After, everyone stared, but still no one talked to her. About two weeks later, Jordan stopped coming to school. I don't know if she dropped out or transferred. Now I wish I had said something to her. Although I don't know what it would have been.

Fifteen feet from my car, Drew carefully presses the button to unlock the doors. Once we put our stuff on the back seat and get inside, he runs his fingers over the blank column of the steering wheel without finding the ignition switch.

"You put the key in there." I point to a slot on the dash labeled STOP START.

He slides the key in and then presses the button. Nothing happens. And again. The third time, he tries holding the button down. Still nothing.

I'm used to this car, so it takes me a minute to figure out what Drew's doing wrong. I lean over and look at his feet. "You have to have your foot on the brake before it will start." He smells like Ivory soap mixed with a little bit of sweat.

Drew looks down at the pedals. "Jeez, even the pedals

are round. Everything is round in this car—the rearview mirror, the gauges, the seat backs—"

"Someone had fun designing it." Everything in the world is designed. Someone decided how deep and how wide to make your cereal bowl, how long to make your spoon handle, and what shape to make the puffs or squares you pour into your bowl. I'm always looking at things, deciding if I would make them the same way or not. But the Mini? The Mini I would keep as is.

When Drew does things in the right order, the car starts smoothly. The melody of the seat belt chime makes us both smile. When we buckle up, our hands brush. I feel funny that I blush and quickly give him directions to my house.

Drew's careful. I like that. I watch as he checks his sideview mirror, the rearview mirror, and then my sideview mirror, his hands at three and nine o'clock. Then he lifts his right hand as he turns toward me. At first I think he's going to touch my face, but instead he rests his fingers on the back of my seat. Keeping his head turned, he slowly backs up.

Once we're out of the parking lot, we both relax a little. It's funny, but when it was me driving I wasn't that aware of him. Now all I can think about is how close he is. I hear the breath going in and out of his lungs. He has to keep his eyes on the road, but I can study him, his deep-set eyes and his sun-streaked hair. The backs of his fingers have fine blond hairs.

"So who taught you how to drive?" Drew asks, without taking his eyes off the road.

"My dad. In the cemetery, really early in the morning. He said there was no one there that I could hurt. When I first got into the driver's seat, I thought there was something wrong with the car. The gas pedal kept shaking. I told my dad, only it wasn't the car—it was me. My leg was shaking because I was so nervous."

"Maybe it's good to be a little nervous," Drew says. "If you're too confident, then you'll screw up."

"My parents never get nervous," I say.

"Never?"

"Not that I've seen. Sometimes they'll get a call that there's been a huge car accident, or some kid who lost both his arms in a hay thresher is being Life Flighted in, and when they hear that, they both get amped, like they just drank a lot of coffee. They don't seem scared at all."

"It's probably good that they love what they do." His teeth press his lower lip. "I know I wouldn't want to do that."

"Me neither." I don't tell Drew that sometimes it seems like my parents are only fully alive at work. "So who taught you how to drive?"

"First my mom tried to. She's one of those people who brace their hands on the dash and scream and pray and stomp their feet on imaginary brakes." He shoots me a sideways glance. "You can imagine how well that worked out. Then she got one of her boyfriends to do it. He made me go out on I-5. I'd had about ten minutes of driving experience, and all of a sudden everyone is going seventy. I think the most I ever managed was forty. I was sweating so much the steering wheel was slippery." He smiles with that cute crooked grin.

"That's like teaching you to swim by throwing you into the deep end of the pool."

"Kind of like that, yeah." His silver eyes flick over to me. "It's pretty much my mom's whole approach to being a parent."

"And your dad? Where's he?"

He shrugs. "No idea. I've never met him."

I try to imagine that. "Do you know if he's alive?"

"My mom's never told me his name." His voice gets softer, like he's talking to himself. "Sometimes I wonder if she even knows it."

When we get to my house, the open garage doors show my parents' matching blue BMWs. My mom's out on the front step, getting the mail. She does a double take when she sees who is driving the car.

"Just park on the street," I tell Drew.

He bites his lip and pulls in next to the curb. "Are they going to be mad that I'm driving your car?"

"No," I say, although I have no idea. They've never met Drew. They've never really met any of my friends. Not that I have that many.

"Maybe I should just take off." He looks out at the street.

"No. Come in with me. I need to talk to you about something."

He presses the key into my hand. We get out, pick up our stuff, and start walking up the flagstone walkway. Drew stays a half step back.

My mom looks up and smiles. "Hey, Gabie—who's your friend?"

THE SIXTH DAY

DREW

I KNOW WHAT Mrs. Klug sees when she looks at me. A loser. A skinny kid in torn jeans, hair that's too long, and Vans that were black and white checked before they got worn a couple of hundred times. She probably thinks there's a pack of cigarettes in my backpack. Which there is. But they're not mine. I took them from my mom when we were arguing about how much she smokes. Plus there's the longboard under my arm.

Or maybe because she's a surgeon, Gabie's mom sees the longboard and no helmet and thinks "donor."

She's slender and really pretty for a mom, dressed in green scrubs. Her hair is blond, but a brighter blond than Gabie's, so maybe she dyes it. Gabie's mom looks important, like five minutes ago she was making life-or-death decisions and yelling "stat!" and talking about femoral arteries and stuff like that.

"Hi, Mom. This is Drew. We work together at Pete's." I wait for her to say why I was driving the car, but she doesn't. Do Gabie's parents even know about her plan? "Drew, this is my mom."

I shift my longboard and reach out to shake hands. "It's nice to meet you—um—should I say Mrs. Klug or Dr. Klug?"

Although her skin is soft, her grip is firm. "Call me Gail. Dr. Klug is for the hospital, and Mrs. Klug is Steve's mom." I figure Steve must be the other Dr. Klug.

"Okay. Gail." I nod.

"We're going upstairs to study," Gabie says, hefting her backpack like a prop. We don't have a single class together. Her mom doesn't say anything, just smiles again. I follow Gabie inside.

If the twin BMWs weren't bad enough, my first sight of the inside of her house convinces me that I will never, ever let Gabie see the inside of our apartment. Her house is big and perfect. It's not like a real house where people live. Everything is in the right place; there's nothing left out—no candy wrappers, no newspapers, no mail, no empty glasses, no magazines, no shoes kicked off. It looks like how I imagine a really expensive hotel would look.

"I'd offer you a snack," Gabie says, "but unless you like baby carrots, you're out of luck. My parents have zero tolerance for junk food."

Just then a man in dark blue scrubs walks out of a hallway that leads off the living room. His eyes are on a BlackBerry, and he's talking while he types. "We just want you to be healthy, Gabie." Then he looks up, sees me, and stops.

"Dad, this is my friend Drew from work."

I step forward and shake his hand, too. The same soft/firm combo as his wife, although his is a little firmer, as if to remind me that it's his daughter I'm with. "Hello,

Dr. Klug." He's a little less than six feet tall and not as thin as you might think, given his feelings about junk food.

He just says hello back. No "Call me Steve."

"We're going upstairs to my room," Gabie says. Now there's not even a mention of homework.

He looks like he wants to say something, but he doesn't. Instead he just nods. I follow Gabie up the stairs, past a series of what I guess must be family photos. The first one shows Gabie and her parents standing outside this house. At least I think it's Gabie. She looks about six, and they're dressed like they're getting ready to go to church. The one above that is just of her parents, I think, but looking a lot younger. The farther they are up the stairs, the older the photos look. They start out in color and then go to black-and-white. Toward the end, I think they might be daguerreotypes, or whatever they called photos 150 years ago. Each one is more stiff and formal than the last. The final portrait shows a family staring at the camera. The men all wear weird white high collars with a sort of bow tie. The women wear long gathered dresses. One of them holds a portrait of a little boy on her lap.

"That's my great-great-grandmother," Gabie says when she sees me looking. "The painting's of her son. He died two years before, but she wanted him to be remembered."

I follow her down the hall.

Gabie's room is the only room in the house that looks lived in. The twin bed isn't made. On the floor next to it is a paperback, open to the page she was on when she put it down. On one wall is a huge canvas covered with headlines and images cut from magazines. At first glance I see

"Fever," "Underground Girl," "It's Pure Adrenaline," and "Your Head Would Probably Explode." There are girls in crazy clothes, pictures of Wonder Woman cut from a comic book, a photo from a newspaper of a man holding a knife, and dozens of eyes, just eyes with no faces. The whole effect is kind of disturbing.

I like it.

On another wall is a poster from the band Flea Market Parade, which surprises me. I love their music, but it's dark. Songs about longing and suicide and memories that you can't change. I tap on the lead singer's face. He's wearing suspenders, and the circles under his eyes are so dark they almost look like makeup. "I like their music, but not that many people have heard of them," I say.

"I'm pretty sure neither one of us is 'many people,'" she says.

I turn the chair at her desk around and sit down. Gabie closes the door. She pulls up the covers before she sits on the bed.

"So now are we going to study?" I say, and raise one eyebrow. Somehow I feel more relaxed because we're in Gabie's room. The rest of the house is like a shell, or armor. This room feels softer. Maybe it's the part the armor is protecting.

"I just wanted to talk some more about Kayla. My parents don't like me to talk about her. It's been nearly a week. They're sure she's gone. That she's"—Gabie hesitates—"dead."

"But you said you can feel her. That you know she's alive." I shouldn't be doing this. Shouldn't be talking Gabie into something that I know can't be true.

"Maybe her spirit is watching us now, and that's what I feel." Her mouth twists. "Like her ghost."

"Maybe. But you seemed so sure."

"But Kayla being dead is what makes the most sense." Gabie's voice gets very quiet. "What do you think it would feel like to drown? Or to be strangled to death? Do you think it would be agony until the very end? Or would you pass out and stop feeling it? Is it just blackness?" Her voice shakes. "Is it like sleeping? Or is it this torture that goes on and on?"

Now the shaking has reached her shoulders. I get up, kneel in front of her, and put my arms around her. It's different than the few other times I've touched her, which were mostly just in passing. Then I was aware of Gabie as a girl. Now I feel like her brother. Someone stronger. Even though I'm not. I mean, she's the one who saved me in the river.

But with her trembling in my arms, it really feels like I'm her brother.

Until she kisses me.

THE SIXTH DAY

GABIE

WHEN I KISS Drew, I feel like I'm drowning, or drugged, or I've gone someplace where things are beyond my control. Like I could fall inside Drew and never come out.

Instead I jerk my head back, push my hands down on his shoulders, and stand up. I walk over to my window. Drew is still kneeling on the floor. He turns his head to look up at me. I don't know what he's thinking. His mouth is soft. He's not grinning, not gloating, not even as lost as I was.

"You should probably go," I say. I don't want to talk about what just happened. I don't want to *think* about what just happened. It feels like whatever was between us has shifted. Before, I was giving Drew what he needed—more days on the schedule, the keys to my car, even fishing him out of the river. Now I realize how much I need him myself.

Except I don't need anyone. I learned that a long time ago. I don't need my parents. I don't need brothers and sisters. And after Maya's family moved away last year, I learned I don't even really need a best friend.

In some ways, Pete's is the closest thing I have to friends and family.

Drew gets to his feet. I turn to look out the window at the deep blue sky and the dark green oak leaves silhouetted against it. I've always liked those colors, the contrast. When I was a kid, I used to lie on the front lawn and stare at them. I could lie there and not think.

Now I think way too much. So much that I don't know what's true and what isn't. What's stupid and what's smart.

I know what my parents would say. They would say Drew is a mistake. I'm going to Stanford next fall. Drew isn't going anyplace.

I wait to hear his footsteps walking away, muffled on the soft carpet. Instead, I feel his warmth as he comes to stand behind me. He doesn't touch me. He doesn't need to.

"Cerulean," he says, looking past me. *Suh-roo-lee-uhn.*

I turn to look at him. "What?"

"That's what color blue the sky is."

"I know what it means. I'm just surprised that you know the word."

Drew's face closes up like a fist. He pivots on his heel, and in two steps he has picked up his backpack and skateboard. In another two steps he is at the door to my room.

"Wait, I didn't mean it like that," I say. "Drew!" I run after him, but he's already halfway down the stairs. My dad stands up, like he wants to challenge him. Like he thinks something is wrong. It is, but not the way he thinks. I can't go bleating after Drew now. So I head back to my room before he can ask what's going on. Drew closes the front door at the same time as I close my bedroom door.

I just never thought of Drew as a reader. But *cerulean* is a reading word. Nobody says it. "Reading words" is how I think of all the words I read that no one ever says out loud. No one uses *scamper* in real conversation. Or *hearth*. It wasn't until last year that I learned it didn't rhyme with *mirth*. That it really rhymed with *Darth,* as in Vader.

I don't want to leave my room. It's rare for my parents both to be home. And even rarer for me to bring a boy home. Scratch that—I've never done it before. They're going to want to talk about it, ask me questions. I probably can't avoid that, because they insist we eat dinner together anytime the three of us are all home. Which is about twice a month.

But until dinnertime, I want to stay away from them and their questions and the looks they'll give each other.

I could read or do homework (although there's less and less homework as we get closer to graduation). Instead, I turn on my computer.

I need to keep away from the Internet. But after I push Drew away, push away the one person who might be my friend, I Google a certain term. There are more than three million results. These are parts of the headlines I find under the News tab for "body found":

- in suitcase
- ablaze in bin
- in farm field
- on roof of apartment building

- by side of road
- burned, beheaded
- in car that had been towed
- in wooded area
- floating in pond
- behind Dumpster
- in burned car
- wrapped in carpet
- wrapped in plastic
- in vacant lot
- in some bushes
- in lake
- buried in snow
- at entrance to golf course

And this is what I read when I click on "in suitcase":

BODY OF TEEN FOUND IN LANDFILL STUFFED IN SUITCASE

It all started when police found the body of 16-year-old Marissa Johns stuffed in a brand-new suitcase in the Houston city landfill. Inside the suitcase, investigators found a bar code, and they were able to trace it to a specific Walmart store in the area. Cops pulled surveillance video from the night Marissa disappeared, and, sure enough, they spotted a man buying the suitcase that held Marissa's body. Police identified the man as Alberto Rodriguez III, a neighbor of Marissa's, and arrested him.

THE SEVENTH DAY

KAYLA

"YOU'RE MY MASTER," I told him after he knocked me to the floor.

And at that moment, I split apart. There's one girl who has to do what he says. The girl who doesn't even have a name. The one who's like a dog that's been beaten so many times it no longer bothers to lift its head or bare its teeth. And then there's the real Kayla. The one who screams and rages and swears. She's inside the other girl, like one of those Russian nesting dolls. Hidden away.

"Good, slave girl," he said, and the nausea rose in me again.

I barely made it to the toilet in the corner of the room. It's just out in the open, so there's no privacy. No place to hide. It's not a portable toilet, it flushes, but the smell of it still made me retch again and again. He grunted in disgust, and I—the real Kayla—made a mental note even as I tried to hold my hair out of the way. Blood and vomit. He doesn't like either one.

"I'll be back," he said, like the Terminator, only with no accent. And it wasn't funny.

After he left, I curled up on the bed. I wasn't thinking anymore. I just breathed in and out. I must have slept for a while.

This time when I wake up, there's a plate of food on the floor. The sight of the sandwich and apple fills my mouth with so much water it runs down my chin. I haven't had anything to eat since I gobbled the box of granola bars. I stuff the sandwich in my mouth so fast I almost choke. It's just brown bread with mustard and bright yellow processed cheese, but I moan at the taste. I eat the whole thing in about three bites and then suck my fingers. My stomach is a hard little knot, like it doesn't know what to do with food after such a long absence.

Only then do I wonder if he mixed something in the mustard. The sharp tang would hide a lot. I think about making myself throw up, but I don't.

Instead I sink my teeth into the small red and yellow apple. It's crisp and juicy. I eat it down to the core, spitting the seeds out onto the heavy white ceramic plate.

Then I drink two bottles of water from the bottom shelf of the bookcase. I want to drink more, but make myself stop. What if he doesn't bring me any more? He hasn't replaced the ones I drank earlier. I put all the empty bottles next to the white plate that rests on a black rubber tray. The tray looks like the ones they use at the school cafeteria. Already, the idea of school seems unreal. The only reality is this tiny room with its white walls and navy blue futon bed. I don't exist outside this room. I'm not too sure I exist inside it.

There's no clock in here, so I don't know what time it is. And it's not like the sandwich is a big clue. It could be lunchtime, dinnertime, or no time at all. For all I know, it's two in the morning. I don't even know what day it is. But it feels like I've been here for a long time. Like I've been here forever.

I wish there was a chair I could wedge under the door handle, at least when I'm asleep. I can't keep him out of here or I won't get any more food. But I don't like waking up to him standing over me. That's the worst.

And I don't like waking up and figuring out he's been here without my knowing. Maybe I could drag the bookcase over. I'll have to try later. Right now I don't feel strong enough to lift the TV down and empty out the shelves.

The TV! If I can find a news broadcast, I might be able to hear about how they're looking for me, figure out what they know. I want to hear my name. I want to hear they're closing in.

I press the On button. But there's no cable leading from the back, just the power cord. I click through the channels one by one. All I see and hear is static. In between the buzz and pops, I think I can almost hear words. Almost.

Maybe.

I think.

But I never hear words that sound like Kayla Cutler.

EVIDENTIARY SEARCH WARRANT

The place to be searched is the residence of the suspected party, Cody Renfrew, located at 5702 SE Eagle Drive, Portland. The residence is a single-family home, white with blue trim, and is the last house on the left on Hazelfern, the front door of which faces north. The vehicle to be searched also belongs to the suspected party. The vehicle is a brown (previously white) Toyota pickup, registered in the state of Oregon with license plate NWE 530.

To ascertain if there is at said suspected premises and vehicle items constituting evidence of an offense, to wit:

Evidence concerning an investigation of the crime of murder, including, but not limited to, the human remains of Kayla Cutler, blood, physiological fluids and secretions, hair, fibers, fingerprints, palm prints, footprints, shoe prints, shoes, clothing and other garments, weapons, cutting instruments and tools, rope or other restraining devices, blunt force instruments, or items containing traces of any of the preceding articles.

THE SEVENTH DAY

DREW

I GO THROUGH my classes like a zombie. In English, Mrs. Lorton goes on and on about symbolism. I do what I do best. I keep my head down and don't attract attention.

Why did Gabie kiss me? Why did she push me away?

Was it only because I was there, someone to hold her when she was shaking? And did she push me away when she remembered it was really only me, Drew Lyle, the straight-C stoner?

I've kissed girls before, of course. Behind our house there's a huge park. Part of it has been left wild, cut off from the rest by a narrow stream. It has a hundred or so old tall fir trees, but no tennis courts, no paths, no playground. Just soft needles. Nobody walks dogs or pushes baby strollers through it. It's its own little forest. Some kids hang out there after school and get stoned. Maybe do a few more things after dark.

The only time I saw an adult there was when this yellow Lab came tearing through the woods, eyes rolling, mouth clenched around a neon tennis ball. Then twenty seconds later, some older guy in running clothes burst in after her. He was yelling, "Bella, come back here!" His eyes went wide when he realized he wasn't alone. He yelled out, "Bella, come!" and then pushed his way back out without saying a single word to us.

But yeah, I've kissed a girl or two there. When it's dark, and you just need to hold on to someone because she's warm and her mouth is soft. But that's not why I kissed Gabie.

Or technically, kissed Gabie back.

That's what I don't understand. What happened wasn't my idea, but when she pushed me away, she acted like it was.

And there's something else, something that hurts so much I don't even want to think about it. What Gabie said, the look on her face, when I talked about the color of the sky.

After an eternity, the bell rings and school is out. At my locker, I grab my longboard and then push down the endless corridor. Finally I'm outside, away from the noise of people marching along like ants, one behind the next. I drop my board and skate down the sidewalk, carving to the left and right to avoid clumps of people. At the intersection, I just go on through against the light. I've timed it right so I can slip between the cars. But some old lady in a big maroon-colored Lincoln gets nervous. Instead of keeping to the same speed, she hits the brakes. I have to brace myself on her trunk to make it around the back of her car. Her window is open, and she yells, "Punk kids!"

But I'm already across by the time she starts yelling, and all I can think about is seeing Gabie at Pete's. Will she even show? Will she still let me use her car? What if she's there but changes her mind about me driving the Mini? Because no matter what's going on between us, I don't think it would be a good idea for her—or any girl—to make deliveries now. I know Pete said no girls, but he can't work days and nights, and Gabie is stubborn enough to do things her own way.

I think of the guy's voice on the phone. "Is the girl in the Mini Cooper making deliveries tonight?" For a split second, some memory flashes through my brain, some time when I've heard that voice before. But it's gone before I can pin it down. I'm the only one who talked to the guy who did it, but I'm no use to Kayla, wherever she is now.

I'm walking toward the back door when Gabie's car pulls into a parking space. I watch her get out. My throat feels like I've swallowed a big, rubbery chunk of mozzarella.

"Hey," I say.

She looks at me, then looks away. "Listen, about what happened yesterday—"

"I don't want to talk about it." I'm not ready for her excuses. Her pity.

She touches my wrist. It's seventy degrees outside, but I shiver. She takes her hand away and rubs a spot in the center of her forehead. Because Gabie's eyes are closed, I can look at her. Her nose has a little bump in it at the bridge.

"Look," she starts again, "when I was crying and you were holding me, it felt right. But kissing you just made me confused."

"I said I don't want to talk about it." I don't want to

hear about what's wrong with me, what's wrong with the idea of me plus her.

She opens her eyes. "Okay. Last night I went online and looked at all these stories about people who went missing and where their bodies finally turned up. And I tried to think about Kayla being in the river. You know, dead."

I don't want to talk about this either. But I imagine Kayla drifting downstream. Her face a pale smudge under the water. Her dark hair tangled as seaweed.

Gabie reaches for my wrist again, but this time she grabs it so hard I wince. "But she's not dead, Drew. I know she's not."

"You're the smart one," I tell her. I don't have to say "not me," but I know she hears it. "You heard what Pete said about the rock with blood on it. You saw where it happened. What are the chances she's alive?" I watch Gabie's eyebrows pull down, her eyes narrow. "You were in the river. You felt how fast it was. How cold. Even if that guy didn't put her in the river, even if he took her someplace else, it was probably only to bury her." I hesitate and then say, "I liked Kayla too—we all did." Gabie's eyes bore into me. Today they're definitely green, and as cold as cat's eye marbles. "Do," I correct myself. "Do. But you're driving yourself crazy."

Of course I think about Kayla too. I want to dream about her. Just to see her again. A dream where it's ordinary, where nothing bad ever happened. Maybe we'll be working together, and she'll smile. That's all. And in that dream world, I didn't take the order, or I did take it and then threw it away because I realized it wasn't a real address. Or someone else was working that night, and they delivered those three pizzas. Not Gabie, just some guy, and nothing bad happened to him, either. Every night I go to bed hoping I'll see Kayla again when I close my eyes.

And every morning, I wake up disappointed.

Gabie looks frightened. "What if he comes back?"

And I think that's the heart of it. Gabie has to think Kayla's alive. Because she knows it could have been her blood on that rock down by the river.

We both start when a voice behind us says, "Why don't you two lovebirds break it up and get in to work?"

It's Miguel. I can tell he's still pissed that the schedule got changed back to the way it was before. He has an old Datsun 280Z he spends all his money on.

We follow Miguel in without saying anything, although Gabie rolls her eyes at me. Pete's working, and so is Danny. Danny has enough credits to graduate, so he gets out of school at twelve fifteen. It's only four o'clock, but the dinner rush is already starting. Every few seconds, Sonya yells, "Order in!" and pins it to the silver wheel.

The first part of the shift, Pete makes the deliveries. He looks awful.

Meanwhile, I work with Gabie. Sometimes she's at the register. Sometimes she makes pizzas. It's the way it's been all year.

Except a year ago I wouldn't have thought about the color of her eyes, or the way it felt to kiss her.

THE SEVENTH DAY

GABIE

AT PETE'S, I can be someone different than the Gabie I am at school. I can be curt or silly or flirt.

Tonight, I'm more like a machine. I just want to forget about everything. Forget about Kayla. Not think about Drew, even though he's standing so close that if I stood hipshot I'd touch him. I'm glad it's busy. Sonya is barely keeping up with the counter, while nearly a dozen orders wait on the metal wheel. Without asking Pete what I should do next, I yank off the first ticket, open the cooler, and pull out a battered flat metal pan holding a large pizza skin. After checking Sonya's scrawl, I prep it with sauce and cheese. Then I grab a handful of pepperoni and give the pan a little tug to start it slowly spinning. As it does, I lay down the pepperoni in circles that don't quite touch. Only Pete is really good at this trick, but tonight it works for me too. Pete looks over and nods with respect.

Once I've added mushroom and olives, I pivot and slide the pizza from the metal pan onto a wooden peel. When I pull down the oven door, the blast of heat rolls over me. I heft the long handle of the peel, and for once the weight feels like nothing. There's a trick to getting the pizza into the oven unscathed, a quick jerk forward and back. Do it wrong, and you end up with the toppings burning in the oven and the dough still firmly attached to the peel. It's even trickier when the oven is crowded, like now. You have to start a pizza out in the back of the oven, where it's hottest, angling it over the nearly finished pizzas in the front. But tonight my first pizza slides in without hesitation. As does the next and the next.

Usually I would let Miguel or Drew deal with the pizzas once they were in the oven, but tonight I take just as many turns as they do checking on things, popping bubbles, shuffling pizzas from back to front as they get closer to being done. Tonight I don't mind the weight of the peel or the scorching heat of the oven, and I don't burn myself once on the open edge of the door. Miguel and Drew and even Pete have old burn marks lined up on their wrists like bracelets.

As the minutes tick by, work becomes a dance, and I lose myself, turning, reaching, bending, using both hands to scatter toppings when I normally only use one. Everyone else seems to feel the rhythm, too, even Miguel, and we step around each other in the small space as smoothly as if we were choreographed. Sonya rings up a bill and slams the cash register drawer closed with her hip, talking to one customer on the phone while she counts out another's change.

But finally, it slows down. Eventually Danny and Sonya and Miguel leave. And then Pete, who's so tired he's staggering. The last customers have eaten and left.

It's just Drew and me. The rhythm is gone, and instead of hearing soundless music, I remember my parents' voices, how they questioned me after I brought Drew home yesterday. After he ran out. After I told a lie about him thinking of buying a Mini and letting him test-drive mine.

"What's Drew planning on doing after he graduates?" my mom asked as she filled a plate with spinach salad. I can tell she is worried, because she slides the plate over to me without asking how much I want, like I'm seven and not seventeen.

I take a bite before answering. "I'm not sure." It isn't a lie. I don't know. I've never asked.

"Well, be careful. Remember, you're moving almost a thousand miles away in the fall."

I make a face, hoping the sudden heat in my cheeks doesn't betray me. "It's not like that. Drew's a friend. A work friend. That's all. Everyone at work is talking more because of Kayla being missing."

My dad sighs. "You haven't heard anything about them finding her"—he hesitates, probably avoiding the word *body*—"have you?"

"I just know what I see on TV." Every night they run the same senior photo of Kayla in front of a tree, the same photo of her car parked in a police lot. Sometimes they show the divers in the river, or a German shepherd straining on a leash, or her parents crying and begging for information. But even when it's different, it's never really anything new.

"It must be hard, not knowing." Dad pats my hand, a bit awkwardly. "I spoke to Sergeant Thayer about your safety."

"You did *what*?"

"Of course I did, Gabie. I needed to be sure you were safe at work. He told me they think it was someone Kayla knew."

Mom takes a bite of her salmon, then delicately pulls a white bone as thin as a thread from between her lips. "Was Drew a special friend of Kayla's?"

"What are you saying? That Drew is dangerous? He's the one who called the police!"

Anger rises in me, and it feels good. It feels strong. I finally have a place to put all my emotions.

And then, just as quickly, my anger collapses. Mom looks genuinely shocked. "Of course not! I was just thinking that a tragedy like this can draw people together who wouldn't normally," Mom says. "Drew seems very nice, but it won't be long until you're gone. You don't want to hurt him."

Now I look at Drew out of the corner of my eye. It's not that I'm worried about me hurting him.

It's that I'm worried about him hurting me.

THE SEVENTH DAY

"JOHN ROBERTSON"

"HI!" GABIE SMILES up at me from under the brim of her baseball cap. "Let me guess. One plain slice and one Roma special?" Her pen is poised over the order pad.

Last time I was in Pete's, I waited until Gabie turned her back. Then I took her pen off the counter and slid it into my shirt pocket, next to my X-Acto knife. Later, I sat in my car in the darkened parking lot and slid the pen along my lips. Between them. Thinking of Gabie. And of Gabie's fingers and lips.

"You know what I like," I say. Gabie doesn't know the half of it.

Her eyes have dark circles, as if she hasn't been sleeping well. With any other girl—Kayla, for instance—it would make her look less pretty. But with Gabie, the shadows make her blue-green eyes look more mysterious. I could lose myself in them.

"Well, I know you're a vegetarian," she says. "And that you'll probably want a root beer."

"Right again." Everyone knows I don't eat meat. It's one reason "John Robertson" ordered three large Meat

Monsters. The authorities are probably looking for guys who like lots of meat. They aren't looking for one quiet vegetarian guy with glasses who builds architectural models for a living.

"And to eat here, right?" she says, enjoying our game. Thinking that she's winning it. Not knowing there's a real game we're about to play.

Behind her, the cooler door opens. One of the kids who works at Pete's emerges, carrying a stainless-steel container full of pale grated cheese. When she hears him kick the door closed, Gabie turns and smiles.

But the sight of that smile—bigger and somehow more real than the smile she gave me—is annoying. *I'm* the customer. She should be giving me her full attention. But instead she is nearly flirting with this boy, right in front of me.

It makes me want to hurt her. Just a little.

"I'm sorry about your friend. About Kayla Cutler." I resist the urge to touch the side of my neck. The fading marks from her scratches are hidden under a very light layer of makeup. I had to buy five different kinds at Target before I found one that blended with my skin. At a client meeting, I told them a story about cutting down blackberries. Beforehand, I had thrust my arms into some brambles along a road, to make it more believable. "It's been what—a week? Have they found Kayla's body yet?"

Gabie's face goes pale and she bites her lip. She looks even *more* pretty, if that's possible.

"No." She gives her head a shake, her bangs falling in her eyes. "No."

A grin wells up inside me, but I don't let it out. Gabie has no idea. She has no idea Kayla is alive, at least as long as I allow her to be.

She has no idea Kayla will have to die to make room for her.

THE SEVENTH DAY

DREW

"CAN I ORDER pizza and salad to be delivered?" It's a woman's voice, a perfectly normal woman's voice, but my stomach does a flip. This is it. The moment I actually have to drive Gabie's car. Earlier, Pete was making deliveries, but now everyone's left but the two of us.

I put my hand over the phone. "I've got a to-go order," I tell Gabie.

"Well, take it."

"You're sure?" Because I'm not, not at all.

"Yes," Gabie says. But she sort of shakes her head when she says it.

It only takes a few minutes to make the pizzas. After putting them in the oven, I look around. The counter should seem like a protective barrier between us and the outside world. But now it feels more like a cage designed to keep us in. If someone crazy walks in, Gabie could be trapped. Sure, there's the door to the back parking lot, but to get to it she'd have to run through the prep area, past Pete's office and the dough room and the break room, and then finally unlock the door. That's way too far if someone is chasing you.

"I shouldn't leave you here alone. I'll call the lady back and tell her we can't do it."

"It'll be okay. All the other stores are still open. If anyone tries anything, there'll be a million witnesses. And my cell phone's right here." Gabie pats her apron pocket.

It still doesn't feel right. But what can I do? At least having her stay here is a lot safer than having her make the delivery. I go into the cooler to get the salad. Sunny makes it in the morning, so all I have to do is put the lettuce mix in a white box and tuck in a little container of dressing. As I push open the door, I realize the cooler is like a fortress. No windows. The door is at least six inches thick and solid wood. Lying in the corner is a short piece of wood broken off from a pallet. I slide it underneath the handle so it goes across the door frame. Then I try to push open the door. It won't budge.

I take it out and bring Gabie inside to show her. Our breath hangs in two clouds that mingle together. "See, if someone came in, you could just run in here and slide this piece of wood in. Try it when I leave." I push the door open, go outside, wait a minute, and then try to pull it open again. It doesn't budge. And since the door opens out, it's not like a bad guy could kick it open or crash it down with his shoulder.

The pizzas seem to take only seconds. I slide them in the cardboard boxes and put the boxes into red insulated bags. The salad goes on top.

I take a deep breath. "Okay, I guess I'm ready. If

someone comes in that has the wrong vibe, then get in the cooler and call 911. Don't worry about looking stupid."

She hands me the keys. "I'll be careful. And you be careful, too." Her eyes flash up to me and then away. She's standing so close I can smell the spearmint on her breath. She's been chewing gum all night, chewing fast and working fast.

I go out the back door. There's not much light. I'll walk Gabie out to her car before I go home. I press the button on the weird-looking key thing to unlock her car. My hand is shaking. I put the pizzas and salad on the front seat, first running my hand underneath the bag to make sure there's no bits of cheese stuck there. Her car is so clean. My mom's Ford Tempo has seats with crumbs and burn holes from cigarettes.

My mom hardly lets me take the car, so I don't have a lot of experience driving. Not that I'm ever going to tell Gabie that. Plus, I plan on never letting her car get within ten feet of another car. I back out of the parking space and then turn onto the road, driving like there's an egg between my foot and the gas pedal.

There's a Flea Market Parade CD in, playing the "Cage of Bones" song. I sing along, ignoring how dark the lyrics are, just trying to relax.

Ten very nervous minutes later, I park in front of the lady's house. I go up the steps, knock on the door. "Delivery from Pete's!" I say when a woman looks out the window. It should be pretty obvious. I'm wearing a white baseball cap and red polo shirt. Both of them say PETE'S PIZZA in big white letters.

The lady opens the door and starts digging through

her purse. She has the same voice as the woman who called. So it wasn't like this was some ruse to lure me out of Pete's. Behind her, two little kids are watching a *Simpsons* rerun.

"Have they found Kayla yet?" the lady asks while she's still looking.

People all use just her first name, like they know her. I guess once you see her picture in the paper and on TV over and over again, you start to feel like you do know her. Like she's real. The weird thing is, the longer Kayla is gone, the less real she is to me.

"Not that I've heard." To stop people from asking a bunch of questions, I try to make it clear I'm not in the loop.

"It must be hard," she says, finally finding her money.

I have a feeling that if I teared up a little, or if I said something, anything, about Kayla or how I felt, she would give me a big tip.

Instead, I shrug. And get a single crumpled dollar bill over the cost of her food.

"We're all praying for Kayla," she says as I start back down the walk. I wonder if it will make any difference.

Gabie is sure Kayla's alive. But if she's right, I don't want to think about it. Because if Kayla's alive, it's not like she's wandering in the wilderness with no memory of how she got there.

If Kayla is alive, I wonder if she really wants to be.

THE SEVENTH DAY

GABIE

WHEN I HEAR the back door close behind Drew, I touch my apron pocket, feeling the solid, comforting rectangle of my cell phone.

I told him to go. I practically ordered him to. But now I wish I hadn't. Maybe I should quit, the way my parents asked. Except Drew needs my car.

Outside, the sun has gone down. Darkness presses up against the glass. I feel lit up, exposed. Someone could be watching me right now, and I wouldn't even know it. What if something bad happens and I can't get to the cooler? I could try to make it to the back door. And there's the people who work at Subway and Blockbuster. This time of night, though, they might be down to one person each. But still, they would probably hear if I screamed. I touch my phone again.

What if some man comes in with a gun? Should I do what he says? Did Kayla get out of the car because someone pointed a gun at her? But nobody shot her, or there would have been a lot more blood by the river.

Thinking like this is only making me crazy. I need to

keep busy. I start by putting away the least-used ingredients so there'll be less to do when Drew gets back. I put plastic over the metal canister of green peppers. Not very many people order what behind Pete's back we call "green slime"—dehydrated peppers mixed with water. Instead of crisp, bright green circles, they're soft gray-green bits. When I put the container on a wire shelf inside the cooler, I make sure the piece of wood Drew showed me is still there, ready to be pushed into place under the handle.

Usually I like it when I'm here all by myself. Most nights the last hour is slow, and I clean things up, wipe things down, line things up. Sometimes as soon as whoever is on delivery leaves, the phone starts ringing off the hook and a basketball playoff game no one knew about ends and two dozen hungry people crowd in. Then you find ways to use every part of your body at once—kicking the cooler door closed because you're holding a pizza in each hand while you ask people what they want.

Tonight it's quiet, but not peaceful.

I jump when my phone starts to buzz. It's a text from my mom. "Called in for five-car accident. Alarm set. Text us when you get home. ILY." I'm going to be alone tonight in an empty house. Even when I turn on all the lights, there are still shadowed corners.

I'm getting some more cardboard to-go boxes when the bell over the front door rings.

I step out into the kitchen. A guy's standing at the counter. College age. But even though I've never seen him before, something tells me there's no way he goes to college. He's a couple of inches taller than me, skinny, dressed in jeans and a black T-shirt, with dark hair and eyes. It's his eyes that get me—so deeply shadowed it's like he hasn't slept for days. I try to smile at him, but it gets stuck somewhere inside me. The corners of my lips pull up, and that's all.

"Can I help you?" I hang back. I'm closer to the cooler than the counter. I'm probably paranoid, but I don't want to get any nearer. He could reach out and grab my wrist.

He puts both hands flat on the counter, right next to the bowl of pastel mints. "Do you know where Kayla is?" His face is sweaty, his cheeks hollow, his bottom teeth a yellow-brown jumble.

"What?" I take a step back. In two more steps, I can be inside the cooler.

"You've got to help me." His voice is ragged. He lifts one hand to his mouth and starts to nibble on his thumbnail with those brown teeth. "Do you know where she is?" His eyes dart as if he sees things I can't.

"Nobody knows where she is. They found her car down by the river." I think of something. "Are you who Kayla was supposed to go out with that Friday?" Although there's no way her face got that soft look for this guy.

He lifts his arms like he's trying to surrender, then waves his hands as if to say, *Back off!* "I don't even know her. Why does everyone keep thinking I know her? It's all lies! They keep trying to pin this on me, but I've got nothing to do with it!"

Pin it on him? Crap. So much for thinking I can read this guy. It sounds like he knows more than I do. And if "they" keep trying to pin this on him, could they be right?

I'm still deciding what to do—hide in the cooler and

call the police from there? ask him to leave and hope he does?—when the front door opens and Drew runs in.

"Is everything okay, Gabie?" Drew asks me the question, but he only looks at the guy.

"Yeah, yeah, don't worry, I was just leaving," the guy says, jerking open the door. Neither of us says anything as he hurries outside, still chewing his thumbnail.

"Who was that?" Drew asks.

I don't know what to answer. Is this guy the hunter . . . or the hunted?

THE SEVENTH DAY

DREW

DRIVING TO the parking lot, I see a man at the counter, waving his arms in the air. Oh, crap! Panic shoots up my spine. Gabie is standing halfway between the counter and the cooler. I jerk the wheel and pull in next to a brown pickup. It only takes a second to remember how to turn off the car, but it feels like an eternity. Finally, I run inside, my heart jackhammering in my chest.

The guy jumps when he sees me and says he was just leaving. Then he's out the door.

"Who was that?" I ask Gabie, staring after him. We watch him get into the pickup, reverse at high speed, and then race out of the parking lot.

"I have no idea," she says. "He wanted to know where Kayla was."

I'm surprised. "Kayla knows him?" I don't take my eyes off the pickup until it's out of sight. Then I realize I should have looked at the license plate number.

Gabie takes a shaky breath. "That's the thing. I don't think so."

"So he's just one of those weird people who only come into Pete's so they can ask about her?"

Her mouth twists. "It was more than that. He said people were trying to pin it on him. Kayla's disappearance."

Is he the guy who did it? I know one thing for sure. "That guy's a tweaker," I tell Gabie. "Sometimes they get paranoid."

"What?" Gabie's eyes go wide. "Like, he's on drugs?"

"Meth."

I'm afraid she's going to ask how I know, but instead she says, "Should I call Sergeant Thayer?"

I scrub my face with my hands. "Do you think that guy actually knows anything about what happened to Kayla?"

Gabie closes her eyes, but they still move underneath her lids. She opens them and says, "No. It was like he wanted *me* to tell him what happened. He said everyone keeps thinking he knows her, but he doesn't. And his pickup's not white, like the one the cops said they were looking for."

I remember something that barely registered. The paint on the pickup was flat, not shiny, and looked like it had come from a spray can. "Yeah, but the paint job was weird. Like he did it himself."

"You mean like he tried to change the color?" She presses her hand against her mouth. "Do you think it could have been white before?"

"I don't know. Maybe." I try to decide if that makes a difference.

"He was scared," Gabie says softly.

I should go outside, move her car to the employee parking area, and come in the back door. But I don't want to leave Gabie alone, even for a minute. Instead I hop up on the counter, turn around, and jump down on the other side.

Closer to Gabie, I see how she's quivering. A fine tremble washes over her in waves. Each one makes her shoulders hunch.

"*You* must have been scared," I say.

I want to hold her, run my hand over the back of her head and down her spine, try to get her to relax. Instead I just put one hand on her shoulder. That's all I need to do. The next second she's in my arms, talking into the crook of my neck. Her face is warm and wet.

"I kept thinking he could jump over the counter the way you just did."

I tell myself that Gabie is only hanging on to me because she's scared. I pat her on the back, but it's awkward, not smooth and soothing the way I imagined it. "I'm going to tell Pete we have to have three people on all the time until they find who did it. Or that we have to stop making deliveries if there's only two on. There's no way I'm leaving you alone again." The clock on the wall shows that it's almost nine thirty. I make an executive decision. "Let's finish putting everything away and go. Even if it's not ten when we're done."

She takes a deep, sniffly breath. I try to ignore how her breasts rise against my chest. Then she lets go and takes a step back. She lifts her apron and wipes her eyes. "That sounds good."

We finish putting away the canisters. Gabie sweeps the floor while I roll all the leftover skins together and then leave them in the cooler for Sunny. When Sunny opens tomorrow, she'll roll the fresh dough first and then spread the reroll on top. Then she'll send the whole thing through the sheeter until you can't tell old from new.

If only it was that easy in real life to make old things new again.

We lock the back door and go out the front, which feels weird.

"I like your skateboard," she says, as I let it drop to the ground.

"It's not a skateboard, it's a longboard." I put my foot on it. "Skateboards are for tricks. Longboards are for travel."

"Do you want me to give you a ride home?"

"That's okay." Gabie's given me too many things lately.

She hesitates and then says in a rush "Actually, would you mind coming home with me and checking out the house?" She looks at the ground. "My mom sent me a text saying they had to go into surgery tonight. If you could make sure there's no bogeyman hiding in the corners, I might be able to go to sleep."

Chances are my place is empty too.

Which is why I say yes.

THE SEVENTH DAY

GABIE

IT'S FIFTEEN MINUTES before closing when we leave. Drew slides his longboard into the back seat, and we drive off, not talking as we listen to Flea Market Parade sing about bad dreams. I'm still shaking, but not nearly as much as I would be if I were by myself. I can't stand the idea of being alone. Alone with my thoughts.

"The police must have had a reason to talk to that guy," I finally say. "Assuming he's not completely nuts about them talking to him at all. You said you hadn't seen him before, but was his voice familiar?"

Drew stares out at the darkness. "He's not the guy who called, if that's what you mean. I still can't remember what that guy sounded like, but it wasn't like this guy."

"So how did you know he uses meth?" I wonder if *uses* is the right word. Maybe it's *takes* or *smokes* or something else.

"Because of his teeth." He hesitates. "My mom has some, um, friends that use it. They get skinny like that. Eat sweet stuff all day and never brush their teeth. They're always anxious. And they never stop talking. Then after a while, they get paranoid. They don't trust anyone, not even their friends."

"So are they ever violent?" I try to imagine the guy hitting Kayla with a rock.

"Sometimes. Sometimes they're just confused." Drew sucks in his breath like he's going to say something more, but then he's quiet for a long time. Finally, in a rush he says, "Do you want to know the truth, Gabie?" There's an edge of anger to his voice. "Do you really want to know the truth?"

Suddenly I'm not all that sure that I do. "Tell me," I say.

But Drew's silent, like he's rethinking it. Then he says softly, "My life isn't like yours, okay?"

Is Drew saying he uses meth? I know he sells pot, but I feel sick thinking there's more to it than that. My parents are always complaining about the drug users they see in the hospital. They get in horrible, stupid accidents or walk away from accidents they caused that leave other people in wheelchairs. And they steal everything.

"What do you mean?" My hands tighten on the wheel.

"I don't live in the perfect house, and I don't have the perfect parents with the perfect matching Beemers. My life isn't anything like that."

I flush. He's making fun of me. Then I realize Drew's not focused on me. He's focused on himself.

"I know some people think I'm white trash," he continues. "You know what? It's true. My clothes are old. I live in a crappy apartment. I'm lucky if I get Cs. I'm not in the AP classes, that's for sure. And my parents are certainly not doctors." He lifts his chin. "I already told you that I don't know who my dad is. My mom, well, my mom has her own problems. It's not just my mom's *friends* who are tweakers." His voice is so soft it's hard to hear it. "Up until six months ago, my mom was working at Thriftway. You know, as a checker. Green apron, white name tag, and her feet always hurt. It wasn't a great job, but she never graduated high school, so it was pretty good. But then she met this guy, this customer. Named Gary. And Gary started making a point of coming through her register. And she was all flattered." He blows air out through his lips. "So then he asked her out. But when she came home that night, I could tell something was wrong. She was talking a mile a minute. And she never went to bed." His eyes flash over to mine.

"So it was meth?" I can't imagine my parents using. Their bodies are temples. Everything that goes inside them is weighed and measured and full of nutrients.

"I started finding rolled-up dollar bills around. And little mirrors with residue on them. A few months ago I found a tiny Baggie full of powder in the kitchen drawer."

"What did you do?" Pulling up in front of my house, I shut off the car, then turned to face Drew.

"I flushed it." He bites his lip.

"And then what happened?"

"She went ballistic. I wasn't thinking of where she got the money to buy it. Although where else was she going to get it? The first time her till didn't balance, her boss believed her when she said she had rung something up wrong. The second time, he put her on probation. The third time, he fired her. My mom used to be smart, not

134

just street-smart, but book-smart. She had to drop out of high school when she had me, but she still liked to do crossword puzzles and stuff like that. She read a lot. But now the things she says and does don't make any sense. She liked it at first because she lost weight. Now she's so scrawny. Her arms and legs are like twigs." His voice sinks to a whisper. "I feel like I'm watching her die."

"What can you do?"

"I called a hotline last week. They said there wasn't much I could do until she was willing to change." His voice roughens. "She's living on Michelob Light and these cream curl honey buns. And since they banned her from Thriftway, she makes *me* go in to buy them. Everyone knows me. I practically grew up there. Do you know how hard that is? They either make a point of saying something to me or a point of looking away. Or they watch me. Like I'm a thief, too."

A lightbulb goes on. If his mom's not working, how do they live? "So that's why you want to work so many hours."

He doesn't answer, just gets out of the car. We walk up to the front door together.

I unlock the door, and the alarm starts to beep. I hurry inside and punch in the code. When I turn back, Drew is still standing in the doorway. The light above the door makes his eyes pools of shadows.

"Can you stay until I make sure no one else is here?"

He doesn't answer, just takes a step inside the door and closes it.

After I text my parents to let them know I'm okay, Drew follows me as I walk through the rooms. In each room I leave the lights on until every single one is blazing. I'll turn them off before I go to school, and my parents will never know.

"My parents have some Kahlua," I say. "It was a Christmas gift. They never drink it." For once, I don't want to think too hard about what I'm saying or doing.

Drew nods, but I can't read his expression. "Kahlua and cream. I've had that before. It's good. Especially if you don't like the taste of alcohol."

"Do you think we could mix it with skim milk? Because that's all that's in the fridge. Unless you want to try Kahlua and cottage cheese?" I feel giddy. Maybe I'm finally stepping over the line.

"I don't think I want any, either way."

His words knock me off balance, but I try not to show it. "Do you mind if I have some?"

He shrugs. "Be my guest."

I find the bottle in the bottom cabinet. Even hidden away, it's gotten dusty. The shape of it, with raised smooth edges circling the top and bottom, feels good to my fingers. I break the seal, pour some into a glass, and then add milk. I take a sip. It's like milk mixed with coffee—with a heaviness underneath.

I walk into the living room, and he follows me. We sit down on the couch. There's two feet between us. I want to narrow the distance.

"Um, I'm sorry if I acted funny about you knowing that word. *Cerulean*." I kind of mumble it, afraid I'll accidentally cut him the way I did two days ago. "I didn't even know how to pronounce it for sure until you said it."

Drew's pale eyes meet mine. "Final Fantasy Seven."

"What?"

He lifts one shoulder and gives me a lopsided smile. "It's a Play Station game. Like a shooting game. And one character is this blue-haired guy named Azul the Cerulean."

"Azul—is that like azure? So it's Blue the Blue?"

He shrugs. "I looked up *cerulean* online. That's why I know what it means. Except, did you know it could be used for all different kinds of blue—sky blue, dark blue, greenish blue? Nobody really agrees on what color it is."

"Sometimes it seems like nobody agrees on anything. Like everyone else seems to think that Kayla is dead." I take another sip.

Drew leans forward. Now there's less than a foot between our faces. Our voices are hushed, even though there's no one to hear us. "Okay, you're the one who keeps saying you know Kayla is alive. Do you still know that?"

I close my eyes and think of her. There's that same little pulse that's been there since she went missing. The same pulse that flares up if I tell myself she's dead. But something's different.

"Yes." I open my eyes. "But not as strong as before. It's like it's . . . muted. Maybe it's just so hard to think of her dead. I mean, Kayla's always so full of life. I'm like a ghost compared to her. Everyone knows her, everyone likes her—the teachers, the kids at school, the customers. If that guy had taken me, do you think there would be piles of flowers outside my locker? Do you think people would have to go see the counselor?" Tears film my eyes. I try hard to blink them away, but one escapes and runs down my cheek.

Drew leans forward and touches it. I barely feel his fingertip. Or maybe it's just that my cheeks feel numb. The most I've had to drink before was a sip of my mom's wine at dinner.

I let out a shaky breath. "When I work with Kayla, it's like I'm not even there. No one sees me."

"I see you," Drew says. And then there's no more space between us.

THE SEVENTH DAY

DREW

YOU'VE HEARD of a contact high? I could get a contact drunk kissing Gabie. The Kahlua makes her mouth sweet and loose. After a while, I don't know where she begins and I end. We're alone in her house, no parents, no anybody, and the world is asleep around us. She scoots back until she's lying full length on the couch and I'm on top of her, and for a long time, we don't say anything.

At least not with words.

Finally, I lever myself up on one elbow. "What if your parents come home?"

She shakes her head. "They won't." Her mouth and eyes widen. "Won't. That's a funny word, isn't it? Won't, won't, won't." It sounds like a honk, like a lonely bird's cry as it flies away.

It's pretty clear Gabie is drunk off her butt. She gives me a crooked grin, closes her eyes, and starts kissing me again. Her hands slide up under my shirt and urge it off. And then she takes off her own shirt so she's only wearing her bra, which is white with little red polka dots and a tiny red satin bow in the center. Her skin is smooth and feels so good.

It's pretty clear I can do whatever I want and Gabie won't do anything but say yes.

But something stops me. I don't know if it's because I've never done it before. I don't know if it's because I'm 99.9 percent sure that Gabie's never done it before. I don't know if it's because she keeps picking up her glass of Kahlua to sip from it, and the more she sips, the more her eyes roll back in her head. All I know is that no matter how much I want Gabie, I want to be able to talk to her tomorrow.

"Come on," I say. "Let's go up to your room."

"That's a good idea! That's a very good idea." She winks at me, or tries to, but just ends up blinking both eyes.

I have to keep my arm around Gabie as we go up the stairs, or she would fall back and crack her head. Which reminds me of Kayla. Kayla and the bloody rock and the icy river rushing along.

LUCKILY GABIE lives up in the hills, so the way home is all downhill on my longboard. It's so early there's nobody out, and the light is as soft as Gabie's lips when I kissed her good-bye. She barely stirred. I managed to get her shirt back on her. It was like wrestling with a giant rag doll. Before I left, I put away the Kahlua and rinsed out the glass. The last thing I did was hit the button to set the alarm.

At the sound of my key in the apartment door, Mom jerks her body around.

"It's only me," I say, and she goes back to work.

She's kneeling, surrounded by a bunch of her plastic tubs, all of them open. The floor is covered with kids' drawings and jewelry and comic books and collectible figurines. There are heaps of stuffed animals, power tools, and clothes that would have been six sizes too big for her even before she started using. She's organizing it all, but her idea of what goes in what tub and what doesn't is only clear to her. And there seems to be even more stuff than there used to be.

"Mom! You said you weren't going to bring anything else back here."

"I'm just sorting it," she says with her lower lip pushed out, like I've hurt her feelings. "That's all."

She'll probably be up for the next two days "organizing" her stuff. And it's not hers, anyway.

My mom has become a thief.

The reason they call them tweakers is because meth makes you obsess on something. At first when Mom was high, she had to be on the computer twenty-four hours a day. She was always fiddling with programs to make it run faster. Only, half the time the computer ended up not working at all.

Then she started ordering freebies from the Internet. We were getting junk in the mail every day—a Book of Mormon, a Wisconsin cheese poster, a meditation DVD. But by the time stuff actually came, she didn't care. It just lay around in piles on the dining room table, and then when that got filled up, in piles on the floor.

Then it was like free Internet stuff wasn't important anymore, and she started looking in the trash bins behind stores. Dumpster diving for pens behind Office Depot.

Perfectly good lamps with the sale sticker still attached and the plug cut off, but she said Gary was handy and could fix them.

And somewhere along the line, she turned into a thief. It took me a while to figure that out. She told me she was going to yard sales, but I think she was really breaking into people's houses. Once I found a garbage bag filled with IDs: driver's licenses, credit cards, even library cards. I don't think she did anything with them. If she found money, she gave it to Gary, but the rest she just kept.

She started keeping everything in plastic tubs. The living room got full, and so did the dining room and her bedroom. She even put some in my room. I told her she had to find someplace else. So she rented a storage locker with some of the money she "found."

Only she came back from the storage locker with even more useless crap. It turned out the storage spaces have open tops. Mom's never been afraid of heights. When I was a kid, she would climb trees higher than I could. And she weighs less than a hundred pounds now. So I guess she just piles her storage boxes to make steps and scrambles like a spider from unit to unit. To her juiced mind, the fact that all this stuff is in storage means it doesn't belong to anyone.

The thing is, she never uses any of it. All she does is organize it. That's her word. She just shifts things around from one box to another. Sometimes she even takes back things to the storage spaces that she doesn't "need."

Like she needs any of it.

To get to my room, I have to step over pile after pile, sometimes teetering on tiptoe. Mom doesn't even glance up, sorting and muttering to herself, scratching and scratching at her skin because she says it feels like there are bugs under there.

This can't be what Mom wanted. But it's where she ended up.

Can you really change your destiny?

THE EIGHTH DAY

KAYLA

HOW LONG can he keep me here?

Will I ever see the sun again? Will I die here?

Is there going to come a point when I want to die?

Will they find my body, years from now, and wonder who I am? That thought is the worst, that I might become some nameless dead girl, a stranger's pile of bones. I finger the label on an empty water bottle. I could write on the back, and leave it in my pocket so people will know who I am. Only I don't have anything to write with.

What does he want from me? He hasn't touched me, if you don't count the time he hit me and threw me on the bed.

But I think it's only the cut on my head that's stopped him from doing anything more. That and me throwing up. If he has some crazy fantasy about master and slave, it probably doesn't involve a vomiting slave girl with an open cut on her head. One who smells like old sweat and pee.

I don't like to sleep, don't like to be vulnerable. Since there's nothing else to do, I've been watching the DVDs he left lined up next to the TV. *Sex and the City* is out because I don't want to give him any ideas. *The Office* isn't appealing because I can't ever imagine laughing in this room. So far I've watched the first season of *24*. It's one of the few ways I have of telling time. Every hour of *24* really lasts forty-one minutes, which is kind of crazy but makes as much sense as anything else does here.

Forty-one minutes times twenty-four episodes means I have to have been in here more than a day. I think it's been a lot more. I don't know how long I was asleep or unconscious before I woke up.

I've tried to figure out whether it's day or night. If I could just have that. Whenever he opens the door, there's only darkness on the other side. Maybe a stretch of cement floor where the light washes out, and maybe the shadow of a wall before he closes the door, but there's no clue where we are, no clue what time it is. And when he leaves, the door seals so tight I can't even hear his footsteps moving away.

What if—and this really makes my skin crawl—he has a tiny camera watching me? Watching me sleep. Watching me talk to myself. Just in case, I turn off the light before I use the toilet.

There's no obvious camera like at a bank where you might look up in a corner and see a black box with a lens. But I've heard about miniature cameras a pervy guy could hide behind a tiny hole. I inspect every inch of the smooth white walls, even climb on top of the bed and look at the ceiling. I do it with the light off, too, in case anything glows and gives it away.

I find nothing.

And the meals he brings could be any meal. Last time

it was a roll and an orange and two more slices of that orange processed cheese. Thinking of food makes me wonder if I could ask him for something you'd have to eat with a knife. Like a steak. And then I could sink the steak knife into his chest.

The horrible thing is that I can imagine exactly how it would feel. The "pop" as the skin stopped resisting and parted. How hard I'd have to push to get to his heart. But I would do it.

I would.

I try to remember what they taught us in the Women's Strength class my mom dragged me and Maya to four years ago. I'm sorry now that I giggled through it. It wasn't that it was funny; we were nervous. We were thirteen years old, and they wanted us to yell at this female instructor who was older than our moms, scream at her to back off, with our faces all contorted and fierce. Later she made us lie down on the floor. Then she straddled us and held our shoulders down and we were supposed to buck her off.

I failed at that, too.

I don't know if this guy is trying to give me ideas, but I wish I had a gun like every character on 24. Or at least knew karate. If Jack Bauer were down here, he would figure out how to knock this guy unconscious with a couple of well-placed kicks and a head butt, escape from this room, hotwire a car in twenty seconds, and somehow save the world in the process.

But me? Well, I'm no Jack Bauer.

Still, I try to make a plan. The door and the toilet are in opposite corners, but the space is so small they're really not that far apart. Maybe I could stand on the toilet and hold the TV, and next time he comes in, I could heave it at his head. But the TV is pretty heavy, at least for the shape I'm in, and I have no idea when he'll show up next. Maybe I could unscrew the light tubes and wait in the darkness for him and swing one like a bat. Only I have a feeling that would just leave him pissed off.

If this were 24, the bed would rest on springs and I would be able to uncoil one and turn it into a weapon. But this is a futon bed that rests on wooden slats so it can be turned into a couch in the daytime. I've pulled it up to its couch position, and now I leave it there, even when I sleep. I don't want him to get any ideas.

Only I'm sure he already has them.

NOTE IN THE POCKET OF KAYLA CUTLER'S JEANS [WRITTEN IN BLOOD ON THE BACK OF A WATER BOTTLE LABEL]

THE EIGHTH DAY

GABIE

WHY DOES ANYONE ever get drunk? It's so not worth it.

I'm in the bathroom, throwing up for what feels like the tenth time, when I hear my parents drive up. The soft light from the bathroom window hurts my eyes. I rinse out my mouth and stagger back to bed.

"Gabie?" My mom knocks on the door and then opens it before I answer. I pull the pillow over my head. "Why are you still here? You'll be late to school."

"I'm not going," I mumble. "I've got the flu."

"Steve, come in here," she calls. "Gabie's sick." She slips a cool hand under the pillow and onto my forehead.

"Are you running a fever?"

"No. Just mostly sick to my stomach." I don't move the pillow. She had better not get close enough to smell the Kahlua. Oh, crap. Is the bottle still sitting on the coffee table downstairs? There's no way I can sneak down and move it now.

"It could be food poisoning. Did you eat anything at Pete's that had been left out on the counter too long?'

"No." My stomach twists at the thought of food. My

mouth tastes like swamp water. My teeth are wearing little mittens.

Within three minutes, my parents have taken my temperature, consulted with each other on my symptoms, and decided that once I've gone four hours without vomiting, I can try the BRAT diet—bananas, rice, applesauce, and unbuttered toast.

The sound of their voices makes my head ache, and the idea of eating *anything* makes me want to throw up again. I keep my eyes and my mouth shut tight until they finally leave me to rest.

I sleep most of the morning, dreaming of Kayla over and over.

In my dream, she's walking in front of me down a crowded city street. Even though she is wearing a gray sweatshirt and pants, I would recognize her anywhere, that straight black hair, those long, fast strides. But she won't turn around, even when I call out her name. I try to follow her, but no matter how quickly I push my way through the crowds, she is always just turning the corner.

I dream that we are hiding in a dark place, and she is trying to tell me something vitally important, but I can't understand the words she urgently whispers.

In one dream, she's sitting on the edge of a bed in a bare white room. Her head is hanging down, and she's crying. I call to her, but she doesn't look up. I run to her, but it's like there's a plate of glass between us. No matter how far I reach my arms, I can't touch her. She doesn't even know I'm there.

Finally, I make myself get up. I go downstairs for some dry toast. It looks like my parents caught catnaps and then went back to work. The house is empty. I find the Kahlua bottle in the cabinet and flush to think of one of them putting it away. Thank God there was only one glass. Will they confront me about it?

I curse myself when I remember how I pressed up against Drew, how I licked his ear, and then told him I wanted him.

I did, too. But partly I was scared of what was happening. That's why I kept drinking so much. And why I kept trying to make things go farther. Because it seemed like the only way through was to keep pushing past the fear. To just jump.

I guess Drew didn't want to jump.

At least not with me.

It's one thing to skip school. But I can't miss work. Not only are they shorthanded, but Drew needs my car to make deliveries. Only what does he think of me? That I'm some drunk slut? That I'm his destiny? That I'm pathetically lonely?

Later, at work, he's completely normal. Normal for Drew before Kayla disappeared. He works hard, he doesn't say much, he doesn't look me in the eye. Is he embarrassed? Does he care? Does he wish I would just go away?

THE EIGHTH DAY

DREW

GABIE'S MINI COOPER is not in the school parking lot. Will she blow off work, too? But when I walk into the break room, she's there, looking pale, sliding her purse into a cubby.

"Hey, Gabie." My hands feel weird and empty hanging by my sides. "How're you feeling?" A few hours ago, I knew exactly what I was doing. Now it's like I don't know anything. Should I kiss her cheek? Sweep her into my arms? Pat her shoulder? Hug her?

"Not that great." She grabs a clean black apron from the stack.

I try to make a joke of it. "I should have told you it's probably not a good idea to drink that much Kahlua. Caffeine, sugar, alcohol, and a few additives can do a number on your system." I pull my own apron over my head.

"Yeah, well, I'm sorry it made me such a sloppy drunk." She won't meet my eyes.

I reach out and touch her shoulder. "I didn't mind."

She presses her lips together and then says, "I would never have acted that way otherwise."

It feels like she's punched me in the gut. My hand falls away. So what's she saying? That we wouldn't have kissed like that, so long that my lips are still sore, if she hadn't been drunk?

Her gaze only touches mine for a second and then she walks down the hall. She goes straight to the front counter, even though there's no one waiting to place an order. I grab a slip from the wheel and join Pete and Miguel in making pizzas. But I keep watching Gabie out of the corner of my eye.

Suddenly, things aren't so simple anymore. All I want to do is be back in her bedroom, watching her sleeping face. Her lower lip so full it looks like a pillow. Her lashes dark against her cheeks.

Sure, maybe I'd like to do a few more things than just watch her sleep.

But I've never felt like this before. Not about Kayla, not about those girls in the park, not about anybody. When I'm around Gabie, it's like someone has stripped off my skin. Like I'm all nerve endings.

And now all they do is hurt.

But no matter how bad or confused I feel, I need to tell Pete that it's not safe to have just two people working. Once the pizzas are in the oven, I ask him if he has a minute. I follow him into his office.

"What's up?" He runs his index finger over his mustache. It's so thick it looks fake.

I think of how Gabie acted when she talked to him and try to sound as confident. "We really need three people on at night, so that if one person is making deliveries, then the other one isn't left here all alone."

"I've been worrying about that." He sighs. "I just don't know what to do. My margin is already as thin as a razor. The price of cheese alone is up 30 percent over last year." He rests his fingers on his calculator as if he's already adding up the costs.

"Maybe you could raise the prices a little bit. Business is good, right?"

"Yeah, it's good. But for the wrong reasons." He shakes his head. "People are here so they can talk about Kayla, look at where she worked, wonder what happened to her."

"So make them pay for the privilege. I just don't think it's safe to have someone here alone while the other person is on delivery. When I was gone last night, some crazy guy came in and told Gabie people were trying to pin Kayla's murder on him."

"Are you serious?" Pete's eyes get wide. "Did she call the cops?"

I realize maybe we should have. "We talked about it. I came back while he was still here. When he saw me, he left in a hurry. But he just seemed crazy and pathetic."

Pete starts scrabbling through his desk drawer. "I don't think it's up to you to say whether this guy has anything to do with this or not. That's why we have cops." He pulls out a business card and hands it to me, along with the phone. "You need to call Sergeant Thayer."

ONCE THAYER hears the guy was driving a pickup, one that looked like it had been spray-painted brown, he goes ballistic.

Thayer and Gabie and I are in Pete's office with the

154

door closed, although I'm sure Pete's listening right outside the door. And Thayer is so loud I wouldn't be surprised if the rest of the staff and customers can hear him, too.

"So you didn't think this was important?" He leans right into my face. "Hello? When it's been all over the media that a pickup was seen in the vicinity the night Kayla disappeared?"

"But it wasn't white," I say, even though I guess what he's going to say next.

"It was white until three days after Kayla went missing," he says.

"But he kept saying he didn't do it," Gabie says. "And it felt like he was telling the truth."

"Really? Then tell me who this is." Thayer pulls a blurry photo out of an unmarked manila envelope. An iron band tightens across my chest. It's the same guy. He obviously doesn't know he's being photographed. He's getting out of his pickup on some street.

"That's him," Gabie says. She sounds like she's about ready to start crying. "So you know about him already?"

I pick up the photo like I'm studying it. I'm really looking at the white house the pickup is parked in front of, trying to make out the street sign in the background. But it's blurry and out of focus.

If I managed to find that house and went there tonight and looked around, or kidnapped this guy and tied him up and punched him until he begged for mercy, would I learn what really happened to Kayla? What he did to her? With her?

Or would I learn nothing?

"Have you seen Renfrew before last night? Maybe ordering at the counter, maybe when you made a delivery, maybe someplace else?" Thayer watches us with his hawk-like eyes. "Because he went to the same high school as you, only he graduated three years ago."

Renfrew. I file the name away, in case it might be useful. Both Gabie and I are quiet, thinking, then we shake our heads.

I try to picture him with Kayla. Hurting her. Throwing her in the river.

Then I think of how nervous he was, chewing his thumbnail. Since my mom started using, she's not a big planner. Exactly the opposite. But whoever took Kayla planned this.

And the voice—I still don't think the voice was the same. Something nags at me about the voice of the man on the phone. He sounded . . . smug, that's it. Like the cat who swallowed the canary.

"Yeah, this is the same guy who came in last night. But I've never seen him before." I look at Gabie for a second, and she nods. "And his voice didn't sound anything like the guy on the phone the night Kayla disappeared. I may not remember exactly how that guy sounded, but I know it wasn't like that." I wave the photo. "This guy looked like a tweaker. He could have painted his pickup just because it was white and he was worried. Tweakers, they don't think straight."

"Yeah, well, you would know something about that, wouldn't you, Drew?" Thayer narrows his eyes. "I checked you out."

Something cold traces my spine. "What? Why?"

"All we had was your word that Kayla left here to make a delivery. You were the only two working that night. You could have had something to do with her disappearance."

"No way!" Gabie says.

I'm too stunned—and too angry—to say anything.

"Don't worry, we came up with a witness at one of the other businesses who saw Kayla load the pizza boxes into her car and drive off alone. But while we were asking about you, Drew, we found out your mom seems to have a little problem. In fact, she got picked up earlier today. Someone reported a break-in last night at a storage facility where she leases space, and your mom showed up on the surveillance camera. What do you know about that?"

"That's my mom." I say. "Not me." My left eye feels wet. I turn my head and run my knuckles over it. I really don't want to be having this conversation.

At all.

THE NINTH DAY

KAYLA

EVEN BEFORE the lock turns, I can smell the food. I sniff and sniff. It's all I can do to keep from begging him to give it to me *now*. Instead, I stand up, with my hands clasped tightly together so he can't see how they tremble.

"I saw her," he tells me. He's holding the tray high enough that I can't see what's on it. Saliva fills my mouth. In his other hand is a white-and-red plastic Target bag. "I saw your friend Gabie yesterday. She looked good."

"Gabie?" At first, it's just two syllables that don't mean anything. My world has been reduced to these four white walls, this navy blue futon couch-bed, this TV, this tray of food I want to tear from his hands. It's hard to believe there's anything else.

And then I say Gabie's name to myself again, and it's like I see her. Really see her. I'm not sure how many people really do see Gabie. She's smart, she works hard, but she doesn't say a lot, hiding behind her slantwise bangs. But then she'll say something so funny that you just can't believe it came out of her mouth.

Still holding the tray above my head, he says, "Gabie

was the one I really wanted. Not you. You were a mistake. You weren't supposed to be working that night."

"I'm sorry, master," I say.

I look down, so he won't see me. Won't see that there's still a real Kayla inside. I'm only a few feet from the food, but it might as well be miles. Last time when he saw me start to stuff the food in my mouth, he tore the rest from my hand and took it away. He told me he would not bring any more unless I acted with decorum. That was how he put it. "With decorum." I'm pretty sure that word was on the SAT. Dignified, orderly, regular. Living in a hidden room with a head wound and a guy who wants me to call him master is anything but.

I still have to play along. I can't afford to let him see that I'm still here. Inside the other Kayla. I have to pick my time and place. And I'll only have one chance.

I imagine taking the silver pen from his pocket and sinking it in his throat, the way they do in movies when someone is choking in the wilderness and the doctor has nothing but a pen. What happens if you perform a tracheotomy on someone who doesn't need one?

The pen glints dully in the light. And then I realize it's really a metal X-Acto knife, like we use in art. The kind that holds a tiny slanted razor blade under the cap.

He keeps looking me up and down, but he doesn't say anything after I apologize for being a mistake. Finally, he just shakes his head, his lip curled in disgust. I should be happy because that means he still isn't interested in pushing me down on the futon couch-bed.

But if he doesn't want that, then what good am I to him? Even if he did want me, it's not like he'll ever let me go. I've seen his face. I know exactly what he looks like.

I wish I had been nicer to Brock. He was so quiet I never knew what he was thinking. Until I broke up with him. Then the words came pouring out, but it was too late. Because I had already met Nathan.

Nathan is an umpire. He's twenty and goes to Portland State, and he wants to be a teacher. We started talking after games, and I thought, I like Brock, he's fun, but he's not going to be the rest of my life. I started seeing that Brock was like a kid and Nathan was a man. So I broke up with Brock, and Nathan asked me out, and I was so happy to say yes. And then I asked Gabie to trade shifts with me.

Gabie would be here now if she had said no. And God forgive me, but I would give anything not to be here. I would even trade places with Gabie.

That's how low he's brought me. I close my eyes for a second and try to beam his face to Gabie. So that if he ever comes for her, she'll look past his plain vanilla exterior. See the horror beneath that bland little smile, the round glasses, the tan Dockers.

"I brought you some clean clothes." He holds out the bag. "You can use some of your water bottles to wash with, and I'll replace them."

"Thank you, master." As I take the bag, I keep my eyes down. I'm wondering what would happen if the next time he stepped into the room I had filled the Target bag with water bottles and swung it at his head.

"It's a practical matter. You smell." My eyes flick up, and I see his nose wrinkle. Without saying another word, he sets down the tray and leaves.

He doesn't get that look anymore when he watches me, I realize. The cat-watching-a-bird look. Now when he looks at me, his eyes are flat and unfocused. Like he's looking right through me.

As soon as the door closes, I pounce on the food. I'm not sure, but I think he's bringing it further and further apart. Everything on the tray has come from a fast food place and is now lukewarm. Three bean and cheese burritos, and ten pieces of what look like Tater Tots with chili powder sprinkled on them. It's all salty and rich and good, even with no ketchup or salsa packets. Less than two minutes later, I'm licking my fingers. Which probably aren't that clean. Like the rest of me.

I look inside the bag. He left me a cheap white towel, a washcloth, a men's white Hanes T-shirt, size medium, and a pair of men's gray sweatpants. Also from Hanes, also a size medium. I wonder if he's afraid to buy women's clothes. If he's worried the clerk would wonder why Mr. Loser is buying women's clothes. Maybe that's why there's no panties or bra.

I'm not taking any chances. I'll do it in pieces, to make myself less vulnerable. I open a water bottle. I've been missing being able to drink cold water, but right now I'm glad it's all room temperature. I touch my cut after first wiping my fingers on the wet cloth. The skin around it feels hot and spongy. Could it be infected? It throbs with every beat of my heart. Gently, I dab it with the wet washcloth. Soon there's fresh blood mingled with dark on the cloth. Maybe I'm just loosening the scab and making it bleed all over again. I stop and try to rinse out the blood, wringing the washcloth over the toilet.

Next I scrub my face and arms, finding mud and sand in every crease. I reach behind me, slip my hands underneath my T-shirt, and unhook my bra. Then I slide the straps down my arms and pull it free. I pour half a bottle of water on the bra and wring it out over the toilet. I wash my body while still wearing my old T-shirt and then put my bra back on underneath it. It's a lot harder to reverse the process. And it feels gross, all clammy and cold. I start to shake. I just have to hope my body heat will be enough to dry it out. I pull on the new T-shirt. It even smells new, that sharp chemical scent that clothes have before they're washed.

I wrap the towel around my waist and take off my muddy, stiff jeans and panties. I sluice down my legs. Before I wash out my old panties, I finger the sweatpants. They feel so soft. I'm kind of tempted to put them on with nothing underneath.

That's when I notice something else in the bag. It's a pair of panties. Women's panties. There's no tags on them. In fact, they're not new. They're not all that old, either, and they're clean, but the tag is a little faded, no longer crisp; it's clear they once belonged to someone. That they've been on someone else's body.

Oh, crap, crap, *crap*. Where did they come from? I don't need to be told that I'm the only woman in his life. This is not the kind of guy who is leaving this secret room to return to his wife or girlfriend.

So whose panties were these?

I start to shake. Because I know. *I know.*

I'm not the first girl he's had here.

Only where did she go?

TRANSCRIPT OF ROB RANIER RADIO SHOW

Rob Ranier, Radio Host: Now in the case of this missing girl we keep hearing so much about, this Kayla Cutler, the family has brought in a psychic, Elizabeth Lamb, and asked law enforcement to work with her. Our first guest is Ike Stanley, who retired from the FBI last year. Do you believe in psychics, Ike?

Ike Stanley, Retired FBI Profiler: One of the first things a psychic asks a law enforcement officer to do is take reasoning and logic and set it aside. That is awfully hard for someone in law enforcement to do, because that's what you spend your whole career relying on.

But as an FBI agent, you know, you have to keep an open mind. I would listen if somebody could help solve a crime, Rob. And if you exhaust law enforcement investigation, if you exhaust psychological profiling, and if then the victim's family says, "We would like to try a psychic," I would say, if it would help a victim's family find peace of mind, I would not stand in the way.

Ranier: But that's not the case here, is it? Information and leads are available to law enforcement. We understand the police have been following up on reports that a white pickup was seen in the area where Kayla disappeared.

Stanley: I have no personal knowledge of this case, Rob, so I can't comment. But again, when I was an agent, I always tried to respect the parents' wishes, whether that was to involve their church members in searches or, like in this case, to bring in a psychic.

Ranier: Ike, to your knowledge, have psychics helped solve crimes?

Stanley: I have seen law enforcement try them a number of times, Rob. When I have seen them participate in the solution of a crime, my experience is that it has usually been some type of vague information. For example, I remember a case where a kidnap victim was taken somewhere near Crater Lake, and we were told "You'll find the victim buried near a body of water." Well, you know, Crater Lake is a body of water. And "near" covers a lot of ground.

In my career in the Bureau, we tried to be open. We tried to listen. I know there are psychics who will say, "I have been a consultant to the FBI." But as far as seeing a psychic solve a case or help us recover a kidnap victim, either dead or alive, based solely on information they provided, then I'd have to say no. I haven't seen that happen.

THE NINTH DAY

GABIE

RIGHT AFTER I get home from school, the phone in the kitchen rings. It actually takes me a second to recognize the sound. My mom has us on the National Do Not Call Registry, and anyone who knows my family knows to call our cells. The only person who calls on the landline is my grandmother. I don't think she believes cell phones are really phones.

The caller ID says Cutler. A sour taste spreads across my tongue. I pick up the phone.

"Hello?" I say. Suspended. Waiting for the news.

"May I speak to Gabie?"

"This is she." *Have they found Kayla? Is she alive?*

"This is Mrs. Cutler. Kayla's mom. I was wondering if you could come by the house and my family could talk to you?"

Maybe there is no news. How long can this go on? It's like waiting to be punished. "Um, now?"

"Yes. If you could. It's important."

Is it about the guy Drew said was a tweaker? Or does

she want to grill me about why Kayla wanted to switch days with me? "You'll have to give me directions."

Instead of telling me, she says, "Do know how to get hold of Drew from Pete's?"

At the sound of his name, I only feel more stuck. I don't know what happened to his mom after she got picked up by the police, but it couldn't have been good. And Drew looked like he hated that I was there to hear it. After Sergeant Thayer left, Pete asked Miguel to work until closing. It made it a lot less nerve-racking when Drew did deliveries, but it also meant Drew and I couldn't just talk. It was like everything was still hanging between us.

"Yeah," I tell Kayla's mom. "I have his cell number."

"Could you ask him to come, too? There are important things we need to talk to both of you about."

"I'll see if he can come." Maybe it will be better to have Drew at my side. We might both be guilty in their eyes, if in different ways.

Ten minutes later, I pull up to a corner where Drew is waiting. He's wearing a gray hoodie that hides his face, even though it's warm outside. He wouldn't let me pick him up at his house. I don't even know if this corner is anywhere near his actual block.

"Hey," Drew says as he climbs in.

"Hey."

"What do you think they want?"

"Maybe to yell at us." Sourness trickles down the back of my throat. "I'm the one who traded days with her. You took the order and let her go. So they might look at either one of us and think, 'It should have been you.'"

I'm hoping he'll tell me not to be ridiculous, but instead he just shrugs. Then I remember Drew has a lot to think about. "What's happening with your mom?"

"She was released until the trial. But it's hard to see how she won't get convicted." He scrubs his face with his palms. "Not if they have photos."

Suddenly I feel ashamed of myself, and my nice car, and my big house. My two parents with their good jobs. Does Drew hate me for these things? We don't say anything more, just listen to Flea Market Parade sing "The Criminal in My Head."

The Cutlers' house is long and low, and looks kind of like the shoebox I used to keep Barbie and Ken in. Mrs. Cutler answers the door so fast it's clear she was standing on the other side of it waiting. A gray cat squeezes past her and shoots off into the bushes. Mrs. Cutler has the same black hair as Kayla, only threaded with silver. I've seen her a few times when she came in to Pete's to give Kayla something.

We follow her in. The house smells stale. Worse than stale. I sniff again. Moldy. Plates with half-eaten food sit on the coffee table, on top of the TV, even on the floor.

A balding guy I figure must be Mr. Cutler is sitting on a gold velour couch. He lifts his head for a second, looks at us without interest, then goes back to staring down at his empty hands.

Kyle Cutler is sitting next to him. I remember him from when I was in ninth grade. He has the same good looks and outgoing personality as Kayla, so even when I was a freshman and he was a senior, I knew his name. He must be in college now.

There's a fourth person in the room, a blond woman who looks vaguely familiar. Her hair is a little too long for someone who is about the same age as Kayla's parents. She's dressed way better than anyone else, in a black suit, deep purple silk blouse, and four-inch heels. She looks at us and nods.

"Thank you so much for coming," Mrs. Cutler says. "You're just one more link in the chain we hope will lead us to Kayla."

"We've already told the police everything we know." I try to sound firm, but my voice wavers.

"Is that right?" Kyle says. His lip curls. "If you told the police everything, then why did you wait to tell them about how Cody Renfrew was asking about her?"

"Lots of people ask about Kayla," Drew says. "Lots of people come in who were never even customers before."

"People who painted their trucks?" Kyle's eyes are ice blue. "Their once white trucks?"

"Kyle," his mom says, "we said we weren't going to get into that." She turns to us. "Cody Renfrew went to school with Kyle, so they think that might be how he knows Kayla. How he came to, to, to target her. The police searched his house Tuesday."

"Did they find anything?"

"Nothing obvious," Mrs. Cutler says. "They took away tons of evidence. But I guess it's not as fast as you see on *CSI*. It will be a couple of days before they know if there's a DNA match. But there are still ways you can help. Ways the police can't."

Mr. Cutler's voice is rough. "The cops don't know

jack. They've interviewed that jerk, they've searched his house, but they say that's all they can do without some specific evidence tying him to my daughter." His jaw glints with the beginnings of a gray-speckled beard. "But if Kayla's alive, we have to move now. Before it's too late. That's why we've hired her." He nods at the blond woman.

"Gabie, Drew, I'd like you to meet Elizabeth Lamb," Mrs. Cutler says. "She just flew into town today. She's a professional psychic."

I can imagine what my parents would say to this. *What's the difference between a professional and an amateur psychic? The professional costs a lot more.* They don't believe in ghosts or spirits or witches. Or God, for that matter. Only in what they can see and touch and measure. They've held people's hearts in their hands, cut out parts of their brains. They don't think people have souls. They believe in electrical impulses.

Elizabeth Lamb shakes our hands. Her hand is cool and smooth, slipping out of mine after only the faintest of squeezes. "Maybe you've seen me on TV?" she asks.

We both shake our heads. I have, though. On a true crime show, she told this one family their six-year-old daughter was dead underwater, that some kind of grate was holding her down. She had disappeared during a big rainstorm. The little girl's body was found under a neighbor's bed. A water bed. And the frame—they showed that on TV—was like a big grate. So Elizabeth Lamb was right, even if the spirits hadn't all been clear at the time.

At least that's how she explained it on TV.

"I understand you worked with Kayla that night,

Drew? And that you were the last known person to see her?"

Beside me, Drew stiffens and nods.

"That's a very powerful thing. Very powerful." She turns to me. "And you traded shifts with her, Gabie?"

"But I didn't see her that day. And I don't know why she wanted—"

Elizabeth Lamb lifts one long-fingered hand, and I stop talking. "Yes, but this has to do with Kayla's desires. Her innermost desires. Now, I need you to both sit for a moment and think about Kayla. I want you to close your eyes and picture her as clearly as you can. Concentrate on her until it feels like you could open your eyes and find her sitting with us."

"She did this with us when she first came," Mrs. Cutler says. "And it's already yielded a lot of information that we're going to give to the police when we meet with them this afternoon."

"Shh." Elizabeth Lamb actually lays her index finger against her lips. "We need to concentrate on Kayla now." Drew shoots me a desperate look, and I know we both want to be anyplace but here. But instead Mr. Cutler and Kyle get off the couch and Mrs. Cutler motions for us to sit down. I squeeze past Mr. Cutler. He smells like he hasn't showered in days, and now that he's not slumped over, I can see food stains on his belly. Kyle at least looks clean, but he doesn't meet our eyes. We sit down.

On the coffee table in front of us is a pile of flyers. HAVE YOU SEEN THIS GIRL? it asks in big block type above Kayla's senior year photo, the same one from the cross, the same one they use on TV and in the paper. In the picture, she leans against an oak tree. But something about it looks fake, like the tree trunk is hollow and plastic, and doesn't extend much beyond the edges of the photo.

Elizabeth Lamb steps into the space between us and the coffee table, so close I could lean forward and rest my head on her thighs. Her high heels make my Nikes look ridiculous. Or maybe it's the other way around.

"Okay," she says. "Now all of us need to hold hands so I can pick up your vibrations." We do as she says. Her grip is firmer now, her fingers cool and soft. Drew holds my hand lightly. I realize I've felt his hands on my body, but I've never held hands with him before.

"Good. Now close your eyes." I don't want to, but my eyes close anyway. I wonder if Elizabeth Lamb is some kind of hypnotist, if she knows how to make people do things. "And now say Kayla's name out loud three times." We all do, even the Cutlers. *Kayla, Kayla, Kayla.* Mrs. Cutler's voice has the ragged edge of hysteria. "Now picture Kayla sitting here with us."

Obediently, I start to build Kayla in my mind. I begin with her high cheekbones, the faint spatter of freckles on her white skin. Her eyes, the color of gas flames. Her thick black hair. But of course, I can't do what the psychic wants us to. I can't picture her sitting. Because Kayla never sat still a day in her life.

When Elizabeth Lamb speaks, I jump. "He, ah, he has something in his hands."

I open my eyelids a crack. Hers are closed, her face tilted up. Her jaw is slack, as if she is unconscious and someone else is moving her mouth. I slide my eyes to my right, to Drew. I catch him peeking, too. I'm afraid of getting caught, so I close my eyes again. It's not so much for the psychic. It's the Cutlers. We owe it to them to do this thing the way they want, no matter that it's probably phony.

"Kayla," Mrs. Cutler asks in a shaking voice, "Kayla, is that you? Is that you, honey?"

Elizabeth Lamb doesn't answer her directly. "I see it. It's coming toward me. It's something you can hold in your hands and hit a person on the head with." Her voice doesn't sound anything like Kayla's.

"Is it a bat? A club? Or are you talking about that rock they found?" Mrs. Cutler's voice is breaking.

Instead of answering, Elizabeth Lamb says, "It's late. Late at night or going into early morning."

Right. Everyone knows what time Kayla disappeared. That's no secret.

"Now I am in a vehicle," she says. "I feel like I am being laid down and being put in."

Mrs. Cutler gasps.

And suddenly it's like I *can* see Kayla. She's standing behind Elizabeth Lamb. Her hair is dirty, and her eyes are so sad. She looks at me. At all of us.

A shiver runs down my back. The top of my head prickles.

"Now I'm stationary," Elizabeth Lamb says. "I can't move. The water is rushing past me."

Kayla is still right there. Her lips are moving, but I can't hear the words.

"You mean she's dead?" Mrs. Cutler says, her voice arcing high.

I hear a sound, like cloth tearing. I peep. It's Mr. Cutler, crying. With my eyes open, I can't see Kayla anymore. And when I close them again, she's disappeared. Still, I know what I saw.

I rip my hand away from the stupid psychic and stand up. We're so close I could kiss her—or bite her. Drew's eyes fly open.

"You're wrong," I say. Everyone is staring at me. "Kayla is still alive. I know it."

And I do know it. I know it like I've never known anything else.

HAVE YOU SEEN THIS GIRL?
MISSING

KAYLA CUTLER
Age: 17
Height: 5 ft., 7 in.
Weight: 134 lbs.
Hair: Black
Eyes: Blue
Complexion: Fair
Ears: Single piercing in each lobe
Scars: Small scar on right knee
Tattoos: None

**Reward: $12,000 for information
leading to her current location**

Kayla was last seen leaving Pete's Pizza to make
a delivery. Her red 2005 Ford Taurus was found
near the Willamette River on Thursday, May 8.

If you have any information about her disappearance,
please contact the Multnomah County Sheriff's
Department at 503-555-4825.

THE NINTH DAY

DREW

I STARE UP at Gabie. There's really no room for her to stand up, but she is, her face two inches away from the psychic's made-up one. And she's yelling that Kayla is alive, not lost in the river the way the psychic was saying.

Although the psychic didn't exactly say that. You could also take what she said to mean Kayla's near a river or a stream. Or even a pipe full of water. You've got to admire the vagueness. The psychic didn't even really say Kayla was dead.

But you knew what she meant.

And now Gabie is practically snarling at her.

The lady tries to take a step back, but she's forgotten there's a coffee table behind her. She lets out a shriek and starts to fall backward. I just manage to grab her wrist. After I pull her to her feet, she shakes off my hand, like I'm some dog on her leg. She steps to the side to get away from us and crosses her arms.

Mrs. Cutler looks from Gabie to the psychic and back again. It's like she can't decide who to believe.

"I know Kayla is alive," Gabie says again. But her voice trembles.

"What did you see, Elizabeth?" Mrs. Cutler asks. "Is Kayla alive?"

"If *someone* hadn't interrupted me, I would be able to tell you what I saw. But the link is broken now. I can't see anything."

Everyone's glaring at Gabie. I grab her elbow and pull her toward the door. I guess it's my day for pulling people out of harm's way. "I think we need to go."

She resists for a second, then follows. "I'm sorry," she says to the room.

Four faces look back at her. And none of them looks very forgiving.

"What were you doing in there?" I ask once we get outside.

"I wasn't doing anything. I was just doing what she asked us to do. I was trying to picture Kayla, and all of a sudden, it was like I could. I could see her. And I knew she was alive." She takes a shaky breath. "Kayla didn't look that good, though. She looked sick. But she was alive."

"That's what you said down by the river."

"And you agreed with me." She takes out her keys.

I shrug. "Maybe. But it was more like I just couldn't believe Kayla could be dead. You know. It takes a while for that kind of thing to sink in."

"That's not what happened in there. I really *saw* her, Drew."

"Hey, who was supposed to be the psychic in that room? That lady is the one they're paying to tell them what really happened."

"She was just hedging her bets."

Gabie may think she knows Kayla's alive, but it's more like she wishes it were true. Everyone wishes it were true. But I think of what Pete said about the bloody rock. I think of the churned up riverbank. Lots of things get lost in the river, and the river never gives them back.

Gabie's eyes have dark shadows underneath. "Are you getting enough sleep?" I ask as we get in her car.

I think I'm changing the subject, but Gabie obviously doesn't think so. "What? Do you think I was hallucinating in there? That I'm so tired that when she asked me to close my eyes, I fell asleep and dreamed the whole thing? Because I didn't."

Maybe Gabie's right. Maybe that was what I was thinking.

"Maybe that Elizabeth Lamb does know how to tap into something," she says. "And just being around her allowed me to see, too."

I point out the obvious. "Then why didn't you see the same thing?"

"I don't know. I could just see Kayla standing behind her. And there wasn't any of this laying down and putting in. It was just her standing there and looking sad. And it felt like I really saw her. Like it was real."

Yeah, just like little kids know that Santa is real. It's all about what you want to believe. But I don't say that.

The thing is, I think I might want Kayla to be dead. Because what's the alternative? That someone took her. Either that Cody guy or someone else, someone worse. Someone took her and has her and can do whatever he wants to her.

I used to like movies with plots like that. Maybe not *like* them, but I watched the DVDs with my mom when she brought them home from the video store next to Thriftway. Slasher movies with hidden underground torture chambers. Handcuffs and gags and chains. Blood splattering on the walls, sometimes in slo-mo. The creative use of a nail gun or a rusty saw or a shiny scalpel.

But when it's not a movie? When it's not fake? When you can't push the power button and watch the light disappear? When it's really Kayla's pale skin, Kayla's blood?

Then maybe it would be better if she were dead and in the river.

TRANSCRIPT OF 911 CALL

911 Operator: 911. Police, fire, or medical?

Cody Renfrew: Uh, suicide.

911 Operator: Sir?

Cody Renfrew: I want to report a, a suicide.

911 Operator: Whose suicide are you reporting, sir?

Cody Renfrew: Um, mine.

911 Operator: Hang on . . . hang on . . . hang on, sir, stay on the phone with me. We're dispatching someone to help you. Sir? Sir?

911 Operator: Man threatening to kill himself—5702 SE Eagle Drive.

Radio: (unintelligible) . . . Clear.

911 Operator: Sir, I'm trying to get someone there to help you. Please don't do anything, sir. Someone will be there in a few seconds to help you.

Radio: (sounds of siren)

Cody Renfrew: (sound of gunshot)

911 Operator: Need units going toward 5702 SE Eagle Drive.

SUSPECTED KILLER KILLS SELF WHILE ON PHONE WITH 911

PORTLAND—A loner. That's what they called Cody Renfrew.

Speaking off the record, a mental health professional described Renfrew's metamorphosis from a delusional substance abuser to a man committed to his own recovery. But it was a metamorphosis that seems to have ended in murder.

After two years of drug and alcohol abuse, Renfrew, 21, started to put his life back on track, says one staffer who worked with him after he sought help last year at a county clinic. Renfrew even took the first step toward earning a certificate to become a substance abuse counselor.

But the staffer also said Renfrew showed signs of a delusional disorder and occasionally thought others could read his mind.

As Renfrew's sobriety continued, he began to recognize and deal with his inner demons, the staffer said. Gradually, his disheveled appearance gave way to a more respectable demeanor in line with his ongoing recovery. According to the staffer, Renfrew reached the point where he could keep his delusional thoughts in check and could distinguish between reality and the fantasy world where his illness sometimes took him.

But his recovery hit a setback when the downturn in the economy cost Renfrew the hotel front desk job he had held for only a few months. Depressed, Renfrew turned again to meth, according to his family, and his inner demons returned. Paranoid and angry, he talked about easy ways to make money, including robbing a bank.

Police theorize that Renfrew decided to start small, by robbing and possibly kidnapping a pizza delivery person. Ten days ago, 17-year-old Kayla Cutler left Pete's Pizza to make a delivery to what turned out to be a false address. She never returned. Her car was later found with the driver's side door open. There were signs of a physical confrontation on the bank of the nearby Willamette River, including a rock with Kayla's blood on it. Police theorize that Kayla ended up in the river, which is high, due to spring snowmelt and recent heavy rains, and that it may have carried her body out to the ocean.

A neighbor reported seeing Renfrew's truck in the vicinity, and he admitted to police that he had been in the area that night. The family hired a psychic, who met with Renfrew and urged him to tell what he knew. Instead, Renfrew shot himself in the head while on the phone with 911 dispatchers. In his pocket was a note begging for forgiveness.

While many of Kayla's friends and family are relieved that the man believed to be her killer is dead, others are angry that Renfrew did not reveal whether he dumped her body in the river or disposed of it in another way.

THE TENTH DAY

GABIE

WHEN THE ALARM goes off, I'm dreaming again of Kayla. In my dream, she called for me and I couldn't find her. When I finally saw her, she was so far away. I tried to run to her, but it was like someone was yanking her back. I begged her to stand still.

Last night I heard on the news about that guy killing himself. Now after I go downstairs, I read a longer story in the newspaper. My stomach hurts so much that when my mom isn't looking, I tip my cereal bowl out into the garbage disposal.

At school, it's all anyone talks about. Kayla's dead, and so is the guy who killed her. There are new flowers heaped on top of the dying ones in front of her locker. Someone has made the initials RIP out of red construction paper and taped them next to the lock.

It's over, I keep telling myself as I go through my classes without hearing a word the teachers are saying. Kayla is dead. That sad, crazy guy with the bad teeth is dead, too. He killed her, and then he killed himself. End of story.

It should feel like a relief, but it doesn't. Instead, it feels like there's a ball of lead sitting in the center of my chest, making it hard to breathe.

I was stupid to think that Kayla was alive, I think as I sit slouched in calculus. What were the chances? Zero. Maybe some people would say "less than zero," but as my parents would be quick to point out, in the given example, that's not possible.

This morning, right before I left for school, my mom hugged me. For once I let her wrap her arms around me and didn't pull away. She rested her lips against the side of my head, and I heard her soft, slow breathing.

Finally she pulled back, but she kept her hands on my shoulders. "Were you very close friends with Kayla?"

I'm surprised she hasn't asked me this before. Why not? Maybe now that we know all the answers, it feels safer to talk about her.

"Just work friends." I force myself to be honest. "Everyone at work was work friends with Kayla."

I think but don't say that our work friendship was nothing special. It was stupid to think I had been granted the ability to feel Kayla's presence. To know she was alive.

Medical Examiner—Coroner's Report
COUNTY OF MULTNOMAH

POSTMORTEM EXAMINATION
OF THE BODY OF
Cody Renfrew

CASE # AC-142-09

CAUSE OF DEATH:
Gunshot wound to head

MANNER OF DEATH:
Suicide

ATTENDANCE:
Under the auspices of the Multnomah County Medical Examiner's
Office, an autopsy is performed on May 17, commencing at 2:30 p.m.
The examination is conducted by Dr. Thomas Burgess. In the
performance of their usual and customary duties, Autopsy Assistant
Mike Smith and Photographer Jane Scott are present during the
autopsy. Also present during the autopsy is Sergeant R. E. Thayer of
the Portland Police Department.

CLOTHING ON BODY:
A red plaid shirt from Target covers the arms, chest, and back.

Blue jeans from Levi's cover the hips and genitalia. In the pockets
are one quarter, one dime, a brown guitar pick, and a handwritten
note reading, "Please forgive me."

Underneath the blue jeans are men's black briefs from Jockey.

On the feet are white socks and blue and white Nike sneakers.

GENERAL EXTERNAL EXAMINATION:
Received is the well-hydrated, slightly malnourished body of a
Caucasian male aged 18 to 25 years, appearing consistent with the
listed age of 21. When first viewed, the body is cool to the touch
after having been refrigerated, lividity is posterior, spread in areas of

pressure and fixed. Rigor is fixed in the major joints. The body is 72 inches in length and weighs 163 pounds.

The scalp is covered by brown hair, approximately 3 inches in length at its longest point. The irides are brown with the pupils fixed and dilated. The head is normocephalic, and there is external evidence of antemortem injury to be described below.

There are no tattoos, deformities, or amputations.

The body appears to the examiner as stated above. Identification is by toe tag and the autopsy is not material to identification. The body is not embalmed.

ANATOMICAL SUMMARY:
Gunshot wound to head, through-and-through.

    A. Entry—right temple, contact wound.

    B. Course—skin, right retro-orbital, floor of right middle fossa, sphenoid bone, left (retro) orbit.

    C. Exit—left temple.

    D. Trajectory—right to left.

THE THIRTEENTH DAY

DREW

WHEN GABIE and I walk into the church lobby, a big photo of Kayla sits on an easel right inside the door. It's her senior photo, the same one they've used every place. Now when I look at it, it's hard to see Kayla. It's just dots of ink on a white piece of paper.

The lobby is jammed, even though the service isn't scheduled to begin for twenty minutes. The only time I've seen this many people crowded together is for a concert or a football game. Not a funeral. Then again, I've never been to a funeral before.

Pete closed the restaurant today, and all the staff is here. There are lots of teachers and kids from school. And a bunch of people I don't recognize. At first, I figure they must be Kayla's relatives and neighbors. But then I realize some of them aren't talking to anyone else. Just looking around at everything, standing by themselves, not looking stressed at all, just taking it all in. And I wonder how many of them are strangers, people who feel like they own a little piece of Kayla now because they've seen her picture on TV or read about her a dozen times. They're probably disappointed they can't buy popcorn.

Gabie is wearing a gray blouse and a black suit with a skirt. She looks like a college girl already. Maybe even older. Most of the guys, like me, aren't wearing suits, just dress shirts and ties. Some of the ties are clip-on. I don't even have a tie, just black Levi's cords and a white shirt. It took me forever to find the iron since Mom has stored so much junk in our cabinets. She says she's not bringing home more stuff, that she's going to stop using, that she's going to stop seeing Gary. That being arrested has scared her straight.

Right.

"I look like a waiter in these clothes," I whisper to Gabie. "Do you want me to tell you about the specials tonight?" I would do anything to get her to smile, or even to see her lips twitch a little bit. Ever since we heard that Cody killed himself, that he asked for forgiveness, it's like Gabie's left her body.

She doesn't seem to hear me. But it's noisy. Everyone is milling around, talking and gesturing. And a lot of them are crying. Jade and Courtney are practically falling down, they're weeping and wailing so hard. Even Miguel looks like he's been crying.

An older lady in front of us says to her husband, "As soon as this is over, I want to get home and watch TV. Opal's having that psychic on. The one who said what happened to Kayla." Gabie stiffens. I touch her arm, and we move away from them so she won't have to hear any more about Elizabeth Lamb.

A piece of brown butcher's paper has been taped to

186

the top of a long folding table. In the middle, in thick black letters, it reads GOOD-BYE KAYLA. People are writing notes with Sharpies that have been scattered over the table.

Gabie and I squeeze in to read some of the messages. A few are to Kayla's family, but most are written directly to Kayla. "I'll miss your smile." "You always made me laugh." "The world is a smaller place without you."

I pick up a pen, take off the cap, and then just stand there, my pen hovering over the paper. What can I say? "I'm sorry" isn't nearly good enough. "It should have been me," I write, and then I don't sign it.

Gabie hasn't said one word since she parked her car at the back of the church parking lot. Now she raises her eyes to me and says, "Kayla's not dead, Drew." A few heads turn in our direction.

"Gabie—" I start and then don't say any more.

"She's not dead." Her face contorts. "I know it."

Suddenly someone grabs both our arms. I jerk my head around. It's Thayer. He's wearing a suit, not a uniform, but he still looks every inch a cop.

"Come with me," he says in a low voice. "Now." He walks us away from the table, pushes open a door, and takes us down a long, empty hall with doors leading off on one side. He lets go of us.

"Gabriella, I am going to give you one piece of advice. Stop it." He bites off the words. "Stop saying that you think Kayla is alive. The Cutlers have already told me about how you made a big scene when they had the psychic there. Do you know how upset that made them? Do you?"

He stares at her until she nods.

"You can't live in la-la land. Not when it hurts people who already can't put one foot in front of the other. Look at the evidence. It's not common knowledge, but when he was fifteen, Cody Renfrew was picked up for peeping in a neighbor's window. That kind of crime frequently escalates to rape and worse. He was a drug addict who supported his habit by stealing. He drove a white truck, just like one that was spotted in the area where Kayla disappeared, and later he painted it to try to disguise it. He killed himself and left a note saying he was sorry. You're supposed to be so smart, Gabriella—you do the math. Kayla Cutler is dead."

"But—" Gabie says, though that's as far as she gets.

Thayer barrels on. "She's dead, and Cody Renfrew killed her. And while we may never know where he put her body, these people have to find closure. It's the only way they're going to heal. They need to grieve their daughter's death and *move on*. They can't hold on to a fantasy. I've seen it happen before. People who believe there's a tiny possibility their child will walk through the door. They live in the past, and they don't ever leave it. Until it's like they're dead too. But you know what makes them stay there? It's thinking there is a teeny tiny chance their kid is still alive. It's some stupid girl saying that she can 'see' "—he makes quote marks in the air—"Kayla and knows she's not dead. Just stop. I don't want to hear one more word about Kayla still being alive."

He stares at Gabie, but she doesn't do anything. Doesn't agree, doesn't disagree.

"Do you hear me? If you won't do it for me, if you won't do it for the Cutlers, then do it for your friend here." Thayer points a finger at my chest. "Because I could make his life hell if I wanted. His mom could end up with her bail revoked, right back in jail. And Drew could end up in foster care. He's still seventeen."

"What? What are you saying?" My stomach lurches.

"I'm just looking out for this poor family the way you won't. You two have been zero help in this investigation. Zero. Drew can't remember anything about the person who called. You both talk to Cody Renfrew, but you don't bother to tell us until the next day. And now you're trying to upset her family with your wishful thinking." He reaches out and gives Gabie's shoulder a little shake. "Kayla Cutler is dead, and I don't ever again want to hear you saying anything different."

TRANSCRIPT OF *THE OPAL SHOW*

Opal: Today we're talking to famed psychic Elizabeth Lamb about the missing pizza delivery girl in Oregon, Kayla Cutler. On Friday, the man suspected of abducting her committed suicide while on the phone with a 911 operator. In his pocket was a note asking for forgiveness.

Lamb: With all due respect to her parents, and I hope I say this with sensitivity, you know, her physical body went into the river. But her spirit is here with me now to reassure her parents that everything is all right.

Opal: How do you know that?

Lamb: Partly, it's a heaviness. It's hard to explain. It's a knowing. You see, what happened is that the night before I received a packet from Ms. Cutler's parents in the mail, I awoke around three A.M. I saw an attractive-looking girl standing at the foot of my bed. I realized it was a ghost.

Opal: A ghost!

Lamb: Being a psychic all my life, it wasn't that strange a thing. I knew there was some reason for it. The next day I received the packet of information, including an eight by ten photograph. I told my husband, "That's the girl who was in our bedroom."

Opal: And what did you think when you saw this photo?

Lamb: My first impression was—this girl is dead. That it was sudden, violent, a lot of fear, a lot of terror. Someone Kayla recognized and knew, but not a close friend. You see, one of the things I can do is read photographs. Like when law enforcement has a suspect or sometimes not even a suspect but just a victim, they'll ask me to look at a photograph. Just by looking at the picture, I know whether or not a suspect committed the crime. Or, in the case of a victim, I can often see what happened.

So I flew up to Oregon and I had the police take me to where her car was found in case I could get some insight into where she was. Standing on that lonely road, I had a vision. I saw Kayla in her car, coming down the road, looking for an address.

And I saw a guy in a pickup flag her down. He was real friendly, and he leaned out of his window and told her he was sorry, but he had given her the wrong address. And Kayla got out of her car, got ready to hand him the pizzas, and he grabbed her.

Opal: Oh, no.

Lamb: One thing you pick up as a psychic is impression of trauma or terror. This spot on the road had that kind of feel to it. I literally had goose bumps. It was like I *was* Kayla, living her desperation and fear. When we were at the site, I asked the detective if he could read me the names they had collected of people who had white pickups, which was the type of vehicle seen in the vicinity the night Kayla disappeared. And when he read me Cody Renfrew's name, I knew. I asked the police to take me to where he lived. And the officer took me up to his apartment and introduced me to Cody. When we shook hands, his hand was cold, clammy, and limp, and I knew that he knew that I knew. We didn't talk for very long. He wouldn't say much. But then again, he didn't need to, did he? Because I already knew what he had done.

Opal: And then just a few hours later . . .

Lamb: Cody killed himself. My first reaction was anger because he didn't leave us any idea where Kayla is. But at least we know what happened to her. I'm not God, I can't walk on water, and I'm not always right. But in this case, thankfully, I was able to locate the perpetrator.

Opal: How do you react to those naysayers who say that what you do is a trick?

Lamb: I can't. This is my work. I do the best job I can. To prove that what I do is true, that's a personal thing. It is like saying, "Prove God." If you have a belief system, and you have faith, then there is nothing really more than that. We can learn so much from people who have passed on about love and forgiveness and how to live a better life on this earth.

Opal: Thank you for bringing answers to those who so desperately seek them.

THE FOURTEENTH DAY

"JOHN ROBERTSON"

IT'S OFFICIAL. Everyone thinks Kayla is dead. Everyone.

So why should I disappoint them?

As I think about what to do next, I use two-part liquid epoxy to place the figure of a tiny young woman in the roller coaster, her hands raised above her head. Or below, in this case. She's upside down as the coaster does a 360-degree loop. The other figures were easy enough to locate, but I had to special order the girl from England. She only arrived today, the day the model is due. She's part of a circus set, her arms originally reaching out to catch the trapeze, but she serves my new purpose well.

The roller coaster is one portion of a mock-up for a proposed new coastal amusement park seeking financial backers. The scale needs to be large enough that investors can visualize it. Mentally walk along the paths, stand in line for the rides. But the model can't be so big that it won't fit through a doorway.

Waiting for the epoxy to set, I think about Cody Renfrew. I saw his white truck that night. Drove right past it, with Kayla Cutler unconscious in the trunk. I had pretended not to see him, my hands easy on the wheel.

The Renfrew kid must really not have seen anything, or he would have told the police.

I resist the temptation to take my fingers away to see if the girl will stay in place. It's too soon, and cutting corners always leads to problems. I'm working nonstop to meet the deadline. Because modeling happens late in the design process, I am the one who is expected to make up the time that was earlier frittered away. The only break I've taken was to go to the funeral yesterday. It was hard to hide my smile. All those people crying in the packed pews. Thinking they knew everything. When they didn't know anything at all.

With my free hand, I pick up a color swatch to make sure it matches the shade of the metal roof. I have swatches for all the surfaces: metal, bricks, rocks, trims, wood, siding. For each color you actually need three, to add depth: one as a baseline, one for highlights, and one for shadows. While coats of paint dry, I've been catching naps on the couch. Kayla was screaming yesterday, but today she's quiet. Each time I wake up, I feel a little fuzzy, but once I pick up the tiny paintbrush, my attention to detail snaps back.

Patience, persistence, and precision. That's my stock in trade. The grit of the sandpaper, the right knife or pick, the correct primer, the exact shade of paint, whether it's gloss, semigloss, or flat finish—all these things are vital. There are other architectural model makers in town, but none as good as me. A few are hacks who might use aquarium gravel to mimic a stone facade. The very idea turns my stomach.

I haven't fed Kayla for several days, hoping to weaken her. My plan is to strangle her, come in when she's asleep and be nearly done before she even has a chance to struggle. I've fashioned a cord with two wooden handles on it. I won't do it like the other one—too much blood. And she took forever to die.

Kayla will be easier. And then I'll take her down to the river and let it wash her clean.

THE FOURTEENTH DAY

KAYLA

I'M GOING to die here. In this stupid hole. I'll never see my friends or Kyle or Mom or Dad. I'll never go to college.

I'll never again take a real shower or pet Wampus or drink lemonade or walk barefoot over our soft green lawn. I'll never go to Hawaii or Florida. I'll never hug anyone again or play my guitar.

Or eat. Because he hasn't brought me any food in a long time. More than two days, I think.

When I first woke up here, I thought it was the gash on my head that would kill me. Now I think he's planning on leaving me penned up until I die. But how long could that take? Don't some people take, like, three months to die without food?

I know it's less if you don't have water, but I still have eight bottles. And I guess there's an endless supply in the toilet tank, if he doesn't turn off the water from outside.

Maybe I should have bargained with my body. Maybe I could have lived that way. On the outside, anyway. But part of me says that no matter what I did, I would still end up dead in the end.

Since I realized the pair of panties came from some other girl, another girl who is no longer here, I've prepared as best I could. The white plate he brought my last meal on—which I now realize might really *be* my last meal—I cracked into a variety of useful shards that I hid around the room. Because they're white and the walls and the floor are white, they blend in. I wrapped the base of the longest one with the stranger's underwear and practiced stabbing and slashing the air with it.

And I took one of the slats from the couch-bed and tucked it underneath the futon, after taking a few experimental swings. As soon as I hear the lock begin to turn, I'll stand to one side of the door and swing. I'll have to be careful. The wrong angle, and I could end up just bashing the wall and missing him entirely.

Yesterday, I tried screaming to see if he would finally come. I was tired of waiting. It was like the first time I was here, only I guess now I know it's really hopeless. I stopped when my throat got raw. Which made me drink one of the precious bottles of water.

Now I'm curled up on the bed, with my homemade knife loose in one hand and the fingers of my other hand touching the hidden wooden slat.

I pray for my family and my friends, letting their faces come into my mind one at a time. Maybe being hungry has made my senses sharper, but it's like I can really see them. Mom's blue eyes are so clear to me that I whisper, "I love you," and almost believe I hear her whisper it back.

I even see the other kids from work. It's like Gabie is looking right at me. Tears spill out of my eyes and run down to pool in my ear. I know I'm wasting water, but I can't help it.

And I pray that I'll be ready. Ready to kill him.

Or ready to kill myself, if it comes to that. Because I would rather draw my homemade knife across my wrists than take three months to die.

KAYLA'S HOROSCOPE

It's not as easy as it should be for you today, because you are anchored to the past in a way that makes it hard for you to respond to what's happening in the present. You know what you want and where you want to go, but are not free to execute your plan just yet. Don't let restrictions or delays make you so frustrated that you impulsively do something stupid. Move carefully now. Think twice before making any unnecessary decisions.

THE FOURTEENTH DAY

DREW

THE FUNERAL was yesterday. Today I guess we're supposed to be back to normal. My chest feels hollow, like something is missing.

Gabie looks even worse than me. She said she couldn't sleep last night and asked if I could still do deliveries tonight. I guess every time she closed her eyes, she saw Kayla. No matter how many times she told herself it was just a dream, just a delusion, Kayla refused to go.

Coming back from my third delivery, driving near the Fremont Bridge, I notice car lights right behind me. Too close. I speed up a little. Maybe the driver is impatient because I'm deliberately going five miles an hour under the speed limit. That's because I don't want to risk getting pulled over by the cops. I've got my license, but I have no idea where Gabie keeps her registration. Plus, I never forget that it's *her* car.

The driver stays glued to my bumper. So close that I can't see the car's headlights unless I lift my head. So close I can't even see what kind of car it is. Just that there's only one person in it. With both hands on the wheel. So probably not talking on a cell phone, unless it's hands-free. But they must be on one, to be driving like that. Like I'm not even on the road.

Now I'm going five miles over the speed limit.

There's an empty lane right next to me. In fact, the whole road is empty, except for us. This part of town, mostly factories and empty parking lots and huge metal storage tanks, is pretty quiet at night. I pull over to the right, then put my left hand up and wave, like, *Go around!*

They don't.

Ten miles over the speed limit. Fifteen.

Now I can't even see their headlights when I lift my head. All I can see is the shape of the person in the car. I think it's a man.

BAM! Suddenly I'm thrown against my seat belt. The car is filled with foul-smelling powder. My face hurts. A huge white balloon is already deflating on my lap. It's the airbag. Only then do I realize the other driver has slammed into me. Into Gabie's car. Oh, crap! My hands shaking, I drive to the side of the road and throw the car into park.

It doesn't matter that it's not my fault. It's Gabie's car. How bad is it? How much trouble will we get into? Her with her parents, me with the cops?

I look in the rearview mirror. It's some guy in a baseball cap and a dark jacket. He's getting out now, bending down to look at the back of the Mini and the front of his car. I'm afraid to go look.

I'm opening my door when he speaks.

"Are you okay, miss?"

Suddenly, my insides turn to water.

I know who it is.

I know what he wants.

I remember the police asking me over and over about the voice of the guy who called in the fake pizza order. They asked me about it so many times that whatever memory I had of it evaporated.

Until now.

I'm ten feet away from the guy who called and asked if Gabie was making deliveries. The guy who really killed Kayla, no matter what the cops say. And now he thinks he's got Gabie.

Only I'm her.

THE FOURTEENTH DAY

"JOHN ROBERTSON"

I'M DRIVING BACK from delivering the amusement park model when I see a black Mini Cooper ahead of me. On top, a red and white sign glows. It says PETE'S PIZZA.

Something inside my chest unfolds its wings. Gabie has been offered up to me. How can I not take this gift, so freely given?

I speed up until I'm right on her bumper. Her left hand comes up, tries to wave me past. I get closer. Close enough our bumpers could kiss. Gabie's eyes flash in the rearview mirror as she realizes I have no intention of leaving her alone.

But how can I get her out of her car? Her screaming, the doors locked, the cell phone in her hand—I can't have that. And my gun is at home.

Then I remember a fable my mother used to read to me. In it, the sun and the wind argue over who is stronger. They see a man wearing a coat and decide that whoever can get it off of him is the strongest. The wind tries to blow it off, but the man just cinches it tighter. Then the sun turns up the heat, and the man gladly sheds his coat.

I need to make Gabie *want* to get out of her car. Her precious car that always looks freshly polished, free from dents and dings.

I bite my lip and press the accelerator down a little further. Until finally our bumpers really do kiss.

I step out of the car, feeling my heart accelerate. I'll need to get the dent in my bumper fixed and the airbag replaced, but none of that matters now. All that matters is getting my hands on her.

She's slow to get out. It was just a little tap, wasn't it? I can't have hurt her. We are all alone on this road. No one can hear me except Gabie.

So I call out to her.

But when the person stiffens, I realize it's not Gabie in that polo shirt and baseball cap. It's one of the boys who works at Pete's, driving Gabie's car.

I have to get out of here. Put distance between myself and this kid before he has a chance to think about what just happened. Before he has a chance to get my license plate number. Before he realizes it was Gabie who was really my target.

Before he has a chance to think Kayla might still be alive.

Before that happens, Kayla needs to be really and truly dead.

THE FOURTEENTH DAY

GABIE

WHEN MY CELL PHONE buzzes in my pocket, I jump. Miguel turns his head and stares. I look to see who it is. It's Drew, so I walk toward the back for a little privacy.

"Gabie, it wasn't Cody who took Kayla." His words run together. "The guy who really did it—I'm following him right now!"

"What?"

"I was driving back, over in the—uh—industrial area, and this guy kept—uh—following me real close. He wouldn't go around." I can tell by the odd pauses that Drew's driving and talking. "And then he bumped me."

"What? He hit the car? Are you hurt? Is the car hurt?"

"I'm okay, and I'm pretty sure the car has some damage, but that's not what's important. Gabie, he thought I was you. I was wearing my Pete's baseball cap and driving your car. He bumped the car, and then when we both got out, he started heading toward me, pretending he was worried. And then he called me miss. That's when I knew."

I feel like I'm going to throw up. "Oh, my God, what did you do?"

"When he realized it was me, he took off. And now I'm following him."

"What? Stop!" I hold my hand up like Drew can see me. "You could be in danger! Just get his license plate number and call the police."

"And what? You heard Thayer. They don't want to hear one more word about how we think Cody didn't do it. But he didn't! And if that's true—then Kayla could still be alive."

"Does he know you're following him?"

"I don't think so. It took me a while to decide what to do, so it wasn't like I drove off after him right away. There's a car between us, and I'm keeping way back. His taillights have a weird pattern, so I'll know if he turns."

I hurry into the break room. My fingers find a set of keys in one of the cubbies. "I'm coming."

"What?"

I wait until I have the back door closed behind me before I tell him the rest. "I'm taking Miguel's car. Hold on a sec." I unlock the car, throw the phone on the passenger seat, get in, and put the key in the ignition. I'm backing up when Miguel runs out the back door. I put the car into drive and swerve around him. Yelling, he reaches out to grab the door handle, but he misses.

Miguel's a lot taller than I am. After screeching out of the parking lot, I adjust the rearview mirror. But I can't figure out how to move the seat up, so I'm forced to sit on the edge. At a light, I put on the seat belt, then pick up the phone and ask Drew for directions. As soon as the light turns green, I start weaving around cars, going as fast as I dare. Seat belt or no seat belt, my parents would totally freak out if they could see me now.

As I follow Drew's instructions, I think of what might have happened if I had been the one making deliveries. How my car might be sitting empty right now. Another empty car, another missing girl.

"He's slowing down," Drew says.

"Don't let him see you."

"I turned off my headlights when we went around a turn."

"Is that safe?"

"This from the girl who jumped in the river and just stole Miguel's car?" Drew snorts with nervous laughter. Then his voice changes. "He's stopping. I'm pulling over." There's a pause. I cut around a dawdling car and then push the speedometer to a place where it doesn't really belong. I'm out in the middle of nowhere now. No street-lights, and the houses are few and far between.

I strain my eyes, looking for his car in the darkness. "I've got to be close," I tell him.

"Good, because he's getting out of the car and going into a house."

"Does he know you're there?"

"I don't think so. I'm about a football field away, and there's some trees between us."

A minute later, I pull onto the gravel behind the Mini. I barely register the dent in the back bumper. Wordlessly, Drew points through the trees at a sturdy old farm-house, the white paint so pristine it practically glows in the dark. The curtains are drawn. The nearest houses are hundreds of yards away.

I get out. Drew's holding a tire iron. I only recognize it because my dad insisted I learn how to change a flat. He hefts it and says in a half whisper, "I figure we need a weapon."

Suddenly I want one too. All I find in Miguel's trunk is a bag of gym clothes. I'm careful to close the lid as quietly as possible. Next I open the car door a crack, snake my hand in, and turn off the overhead light, and then slide back into the car to look on the floors and seats. There's wrappers and receipts, but nothing useful.

As an afterthought, I open the glove compartment. And there it is. A gun.

I pick it up by the grip, not putting my finger anywhere near the trigger. It feels serious. Deadly.

I get out of the car and show Drew, careful to keep the barrel pointed toward the ground. He squints in the darkness.

"Holy crap—Miguel has a gun?"

"I guess." I realize I'm wincing, already braced for the sound it could make. "Have you ever fired one?"

Drew shakes his head. "One of my mom's boyfriends had one, and I saw it on the dresser. But he would have beaten my butt if I touched it." He offers the tire iron. "Want to trade?"

I try to think logically about a situation that is no longer logical. "I don't think I'm strong enough to really do any damage with a tire iron. Besides, we're not going to use it. Just threaten him if we have to." I look toward the house and see a shadow walk past the curtains. "Let's go. And if we see anything weird, or any hint that Kayla is there for sure, we call the cops."

Drew doesn't argue.

The gravel is noisy, so we run on the dark road. All too soon, we're crouched at the edge of the lawn. The lights are on in all the rooms of the house, but the curtains are drawn.

"Look!" Drew whispers, pointing. There's a vertical line of light in the big window at the front, a gap where the curtains don't quite meet. We nod at each other and then scurry across the yard. I feel so exposed, like at any moment a spotlight—or a bullet—will find me. My heart is beating in my ears. My breath comes in gasps. I close my mouth, trying not to let the sound out.

Drew looks inside first. He stiffens, then glances back and touches my arm. He moves his head an inch or two so I can see.

There's a guy scrabbling through a desk drawer, muttering to himself. He's about ten feet away, his face half turned away from us. At first I think the room is full of dollhouses, but then I realize they're models of buildings.

Finally, he straightens up so that we can see all of his face. I put my hand on Drew's arm to steady myself. I know this guy with short dark hair and wire frame glasses. He comes into Pete's all the time, and he always jokes with me. Silly, superficial jokes that you forget as soon as he turns away. He always orders whatever meatless slices we have. He's just some harmless guy as old as my dad.

Only what he's taking out of the drawer is a gun.

And before we have time to react, he turns and runs down a set of stairs at the far left of the room.

Drew and I stare at each other. I fumble my phone from my pocket, but before I can even press the nine, a sound comes from the basement that chills my bones.

It's a woman. Screaming.

THE FOURTEENTH DAY

DREW

GABIE'S DIALING 911, but there's no time for that. I should have listened to her. No matter what Thayer told us, I should have called them first thing. I try the door. Locked. I slam my shoulder into it. It shakes, but stays solid in the frame. I try again. And again. I'm getting noplace fast.

Kayla screams again. At least I think it's Kayla. I hope it's Kayla. I slam my shoulder again, ignoring the pain.

Or should I be hoping it isn't her?

Gabie is telling the police where we are, so panicked her words are running into each other. I hear her say something about a man with a gun and screams. But she never says Kayla's name. Which is probably a good move if we want them to believe us.

My shoulder feels like it's broken, but the door isn't budging. Then I remember the tire iron. I smash it into the window at the top of the door, then knock away most of the shards. But the lock's pretty far down. I have to stand on tiptoe and reach all the way to my elbow to get to the lock and turn it. A piece of glass slices into my arm as I pull it back out, but it doesn't hurt. There's just a fast, slippy feeling as it parts my flesh.

Already swinging the tire iron in front of me, I open the door, growling as if the guy is going to be right there. Gabie's close behind me.

"They're on their way," she says, shoving her phone into her pocket. But we both know that by the time they get here, Kayla or whoever is screaming might be dead for real.

"Cover me," I say, because it sounds like the thing to say. Gabie raises the gun to shoulder level, and I just hope she doesn't shoot me with it. We race down the worn wooden stairs into darkness. Just around the corner, I hear another scream and a grunt of pain. Is it really Kayla? All I know for sure is that whoever is screaming is a woman.

"Police!" I shout, making my voice as deep and as authoritative as possible. Maybe I can buy us some time until the real police get here.

I round the corner at the bottom of the stairs. Twenty feet ahead of me, light spills out of a doorway to a narrow white room. It reveals the shadowy contours of a low-ceilinged basement with a concrete floor. I have a vague impression of a workbench to our right. But I only have eyes for the guy. He's facing the light, with his back to us.

And standing silhouetted in the doorway of that small, windowless room is—oh, my God!—Kayla. Her hair is matted, and she looks skinny and dirty, but it's Kayla, all right. Holding a short board like a softball bat, cocked above her right shoulder. She must have already hit him once, because there is blood on the side of his face.

His free hand comes away from his cheek, his fingertips dark with blood. Now he's lifting his gun.

"Drop your weapon!" I yell. But the guy doesn't
move. He's going to kill Kayla.

Gabie lets out a little moan. Just as I whip my head
around to see what's wrong, she pulls the trigger on her
own gun.

There's the faintest little plasticky pop.

"Ow!" With his free hand, the guy swipes at the back
of his neck. The undamaged back of his neck.

Oh, crap. Reality sinks in. Miguel didn't have a *gun*
in his car. He had a BB gun. And those two little letters
are probably going to make the difference between at
least one of us living or dying.

I have to do something, but in the time it will take to
tackle him, he could shoot Kayla. So I shout and throw
the tire iron at his head. And watch with horror as it
misses him by an inch and goes clattering into the dark.
But along with the tire iron, blood flies off my fingertips
and splatters all over the guy, Kayla, and even the walls,
like I'm some kind of crazy Jackson Pollock. My hand and
arm look like they've been dipped in red paint. The guy
with the gun grimaces and tries to wipe the blood off his
face with the heel of his hand.

Kayla takes advantage of that moment of distrac-
tion to swing the board again. Not at his head, but at
the gun. It skitters across the concrete floor into the
darkness.

Now it's three of us against one of him, and nobody
has a gun. The tables are turning.

Then suddenly the light is gone, and the tables have

turned back again. The four of us are alone in the dark—but only one of us knows the layout of the basement. There's just a faint square of light at the top of the stairs. Everyone moves, everyone cries out, so there's a confused jumble of noise and shifting shadows.

"Kayla!" Gabie shouts. "Kay—" Her voice is choked off. I spin in a circle, my hands outstretched, trying to figure out where she is.

I hear scrabbling, and then two dim figures lurch to the base of the stairs. It's the guy. He's got Gabie in a headlock. And his right hand is pressing something that flashes silver against the side of her neck. At first I think it's a knife, but then I realize it's a screwdriver from the workbench.

I look around for Kayla. She's on her knees, head hanging down, one hand inside the little room that must have been her prison, the other pressed against her stomach. She isn't holding the board anymore. Did he hurt her? Jab her with the screwdriver before he took Gabie?

"You. Boy. Get that flashlight." He jerks his head at where it hangs on the workbench. I do as he says, revealing the black flashlight-shaped outline he has traced on the pegboard. "Now find the gun and give it to me, or I'll stab Gabie so hard it will come out the other side."

It doesn't seem possible that my anxiety could be any greater, but when I hear Gabie's name in his mouth, I want to scream. He digs the screwdriver in a little deeper. A tiny dark line snakes down the white skin of Gabie's throat.

He's got her head pulled so far back that I can't see her eyes. But I can hear her voice. "Don't do it," Gabie chokes out. "Don't listen to him." I know what she's thinking. Once he has the gun, what's to stop him from shooting all three of us?

But I do. I do listen to him. Because his eyes are crazy and his mouth is set, and I know he will kill Gabie right now if I don't do what he wants. And I can't just stand there and watch that happen.

There's another empty outline on the pegboard, one shaped like the screwdriver he has pressed against her neck. The board still holds a couple dozen tools: wrenches, hammers, putty knives, saws. While they all look like they could inflict some damage at close range, none of them are worth the risk. I thumb the flashlight on, then walk to the corner where I saw the gun go flying.

"Hurry up!" he barks, and for punctuation Gabie lets out a whimper. How far has he pressed it into her? I think of all the important stuff that runs through your neck, like we learned in biology. The trachea. The jugular vein. The spine.

The flashlight picks up a black gleam. The gun. I switch the flashlight to my left hand, pick up the gun and straighten up. Even though I'm moving quickly, time slows down. My thoughts tumble over themselves as I wonder if I have the courage or the stupidity to try shooting him when he's tucked himself right behind Gabie. I turn around, still not sure what to do. And that's when Kayla launches herself past me with a wordless scream. In her hands is something white and narrow and about six inches long.

Then the three of them are a shouting, screaming, grunting blur on the floor. A girl cries out. Sirens cut through the air, getting louder. But I don't think they'll get here in time.

I swing the flashlight over. The guy gets to his feet, pressing one hand against his bloody side where his shirt has been sliced open. Kayla and Gabie are still on the floor. He kicks Kayla. Hard. Then Gabie. They don't seem to be moving. He takes two steps to the pegboard. His fingers run over it and stop at a huge silver monkey wrench. He yanks it off its pegs, turns back, and lifts it high overhead.

And that's when I pull the trigger.

THE FOURTEENTH DAY

KAYLA

THE SOUND of the gun going off is so loud that I can't hear anything for a few seconds afterward.

Then I dimly become aware of sirens wailing and men shouting, "Police! Police!"

"Down here," I yell, then start to push myself up. My bloody hand slips on the painted concrete floor, and I fall onto someone else. Someone warm and wet. It's him, I know it. Gagging with revulsion and fear, I scramble back. But when a flashlight slices down the stairs, I see it's Gabie. Her neck is shiny with blood as red as paint, and more blood is running down to pool on the cement floor.

"Help us!" I scream, and press my hand against her throat. "She's hurt!" The hot blood seeps between my fingers.

The first cop down the stairs points his gun past us. Right at Drew.

"Put down your weapon!"

I whip my head around. Drew is frozen, one hand holding a flashlight loose at his side, his other hand still wrapped around the gun, blood dripping from his arm.

His eyes are fixed on what lies just behind Gaby and me, the remains of the man who held me prisoner. Drew's lips are pulled back in an expression that's halfway between a grimace and a growl. He seems completely unaware of the cop.

I realize if Drew doesn't put the gun down soon, the cop is going to decide that he might just be the bad guy.

"Drew," I say in the most soothing and reasonable tone I can muster, "it's okay. Put the gun down and help me with Gabie."

He stares at me, unmoving. The moment stretches out. I don't think any of us even blink. Finally Drew gives his head a little shake, then bends down and lays first the flashlight and then the gun on the floor. As the first cop holsters his gun, more cops come running down the stairs.

Drew yanks the red Pete's shirt over his head and throws it to me. I press it against Gabie's throat. She's not moving at all. I tell myself she's still alive. She has to be. I mean, dead people don't keep bleeding, do they?

The lights come on, and we all blink. There's so much blood it looks fake, especially splashed around in this tidy room where the only things out of place are the blood-drenched people. Gabie looks like a girl cleverly fashioned of wax. The cops are barking orders, calling for ambulances, bending over the body of the guy who kidnapped me. One of them pushes me aside and starts working on Gabie. A second one starts to wrap something around Drew's arm.

I stand up and back out of the way. And when the one who put his fingers against the guy's throat straightens up and shakes his head, relief surges through me. It's over. It's really over. My knees buckle, and I almost fall down.

"Kayla," Drew calls out, and I tear my gaze away from the dead guy. Instead I look at Drew, at his gray eyes. "Gabie always knew," he says. "She tried to tell everyone you were still alive."

FIVE MINUTES LATER, two paramedics are strapping Gabie to a backboard. The cops have separated Drew and me. I can see him gesturing, pointing with his roughly bandaged arm at the body of the man in the corner. At the man who kept me here. The man who tried to kill me. They haven't even covered his face.

Another cop touches my arm lightly, and I turn to look at him. He has a notebook. "So your name is . . . ?"

"Kayla. Kayla Cutler."

His eyes go wide. "Kayla Cutler? Who worked at Pete's Pizza?"

I nod. It's clear from his expression that if I had been able to get the TV to play anything but static, I *would* have heard my name, heard how they were searching for me.

"And that man"—he gestures with his chin—"who was he?"

"A customer, but I don't know his name. Just his face. He locked me in here." I shudder. "He wanted me to call him master."

His lips press together for a long second. "And how did he die?"

"Drew shot him when he was pushing a screwdriver into Gabie's neck." We both turn and look as the paramedics begin to carry her up the stairs. Her mouth is slack, her eyes closed.

They've summoned another ambulance for Drew and me, and the cop says the rest of the questioning will wait until we've all been checked out at the hospital. He takes my arm as we go up the stairs. Outside the front lawn is covered with cop cars. There are no nearby houses. No one who could have heard me screaming.

The back doors of one of the two ambulances are open. Inside, I can see them working on Gabie's still form. She's being given oxygen, and one of the paramedics is hanging a clear bag of liquid that goes down into a tube that ends in the back of one of her hands.

Then she raises that hand to her face, and something inside of me loosens. She's alive, then. Gabie's definitely alive.

I take a deep breath. I can smell grass and dirt and a million other smells I thought I would never smell again. The stars sparkle like diamonds, and I start to cry.

LESS THAN AN HOUR LATER, three doctors are standing outside my emergency room cubicle, discussing how best to treat my head, when a cop pushes the curtain aside. I'm lying down. I'm still weak even though they've given me three packs of soda crackers and a granola bar and have promised to bring me more food. Because I couldn't stop shivering, they've covered me with heated white blankets. Heating blankets is a genius idea.

For a second, the cop just looks at me. He has a strong nose and eyes that don't miss a trick. Then he smiles, and he no longer looks intimidating. He stretches out his hand.

"Kayla, I'm Sergeant Thayer. I've been working on your case since the beginning."

I prop myself up on one elbow and sort of shake his hand. "Thank you," I say. It's strange to think of myself as a case.

"I'll need to talk to you tomorrow," he says. "There are still some details we need to fill in."

I nod. I remember the panties that must have belonged to some other girl, but I don't want to think about her now. Tomorrow will be soon enough.

"There are some people here to see you." Sergeant Thayer turns and pulls back the curtain, and my parents and brother crowd in as he leaves. I sit all the way up . All three of them manage to put their arms around me. Our faces are hot and wet with tears. We're all crying and laughing at the same time.

Finally, my mom pulls back and looks at me. For the first time, her eyes take in the bandage over one ear and my newly bald head. The nurse was going to just shave off one side, but I told her that would look even more ridiculous.

"Oh, Kayla," she breathes, her fingers hovering just above the bandage, "your hair!"

"I think she looks cool," Kyle says. "Like some kick-ass warrior." My dad nods, wiping his eyes.

My mom purses her lips. "Kayla's just lucky that she has a nice-shaped head."

The comment is so like my mom—always seeing the bright side of any situation—that the four of us start laughing. I haven't laughed in so long. If Gabie and Drew hadn't come for me, I might never have laughed again.

Thank God I didn't draw that homemade knife across my wrists.

It's so wonderful to be surrounded by my family that it takes a few minutes for me to see how bad they actually look. My mom's face is hollow; my dad's, unshaven. Kyle has circles under his eyes. I realize that every day I spent in that basement, they spent in their own prison.

But now we're all free.

THE SIXTEENTH DAY

GABIE

EVEN IF YOUR parents work as surgeons in the very hospital in which you are staying, it turns out that they don't let you stay there very long. You have to be really sick or even dying. And the three of us are a long way from that. We've only spent a day and a half on the med-surg floor, and now we're going to be discharged. My parents did talk the coordinator into letting Kayla and me room together, and they put Drew in the next room over. After being debriefed by the cops, we've spent most of our time filling each other in.

They've done everything they can to make sure we get better fast and stay healthy. Kayla, Drew, and I have had tetanus shots and X-rays, and we've been prescribed broad-spectrum antibiotics that we'll each be taking for ten days, just in case. Of course, they couldn't do anything about the fact that we're all still covered in bruises and stitches. If you put the three of us together, we would make one great Frankenstein monster.

Kayla's palm got cut from her homemade knife, but my mom said that it didn't do any permanent damage to the tendons and nerves, so it shouldn't affect her softball scholarship. Her head is shaved and stitched, and she jokes that it even looks like a softball. By the time college starts in the fall, she says she might have enough hair that it can pass for a pixie cut.

Drew's arm took seventeen stitches, and he needed a couple of pints of blood, but he's okay, too. My parents worked on him, just as they worked on Kayla. They weren't allowed to work on me, but that didn't stop them from checking on me a million times as a plastic surgeon stitched the stab wound in my neck. Thanks to Kayla's intervention, it's not very deep, and it missed anything important. My parents keep reassuring me that the scar will be no bigger around than a pencil. After everything that happened, it doesn't seem like that big of a deal.

The guy is dead. It turns out he had a name, and it wasn't John Robertson like he told Drew when he ordered pizza. It was Ronald Hewett. He worked at home, building architectural models. And one life-sized room in his basement, the perfect place to stash a girl. On his computer, the cops found notes about every woman and girl at Pete's Pizza, the pros and cons of taking each, and how best to do it. He had picked out a girl—me—and then a night. When Kayla turned up instead of me, he stuck to his plans. I have a feeling that he was the kind of guy who had trouble deviating from plans. Then he wrote about what a disappointment Kayla was. About how I would have been much better. I try not to think about that very much.

Hewett had no criminal record, but yesterday the cops brought in a cadaver dog. In his yard, Hewett had buried a girl who had been shot in the head. She went missing from Beaverton over six months ago. Everyone thought she was a runaway. I try not to think about her either.

And Cody Renfrew, the guy who shot himself after talking to Elizabeth Lamb, the so-called psychic? The best guess is that he had the bad luck to be in the vicinity the night Kayla disappeared. The meth made him paranoid, and then her being missing pushed him over the edge.

There's a knock on the partly open door. It's Drew, his right arm bandaged from elbow to wrist. "Ladies, your carriages await," he says. He opens the door wider, and I see my dad pushing an empty wheelchair. Behind him are our moms—and they have empty wheelchairs, too. Drew nods at my mom, then sits in the wheelchair she's pushing. He leans forward to fold down the footrests.

"You're kidding, right?" I appeal to my dad.

He gives me a wink. "Hospital policy, kiddo." Ever since I was admitted, my parents have been treating me differently, joking around with me. I've even seen them both cry, something I'd never seen before.

Half the nursing staff is hovering in the background, grinning. I have the feeling we're the most exciting patients they've had in a long time. We got so many flowers we asked that they give them to other patients in the hospital. And we've had interview requests from every TV show and newspaper. But we just say no. Kayla and Drew and I talked about it the first night and decided we didn't need to share everything with the world.

My dad pushes the wheelchair to the edge of the bed. "Come on. Kayla's dad is out by the loading dock, and our car is, too. We need to get out of here before the media figures out what's going on."

"I guess you guys are on delivery tonight," Kayla says.

Of course, my parents and Kayla's mom have never worked at Pete's, so it goes right over their heads. But Drew and Kayla and I look at each other. We don't smile—we don't have to. We know how much we owe each other, how close we all came to death.

"Then I guess it's order up!" I say, settling into the wheelchair. "Three mediums with the works."

Kayla gets in her own chair and makes a fake frowny face at me. "Speak for yourself, missy. I'm a small."

THE EIGHTY-EIGHTH DAY

DREW

IF YOU HAD told me that I would ever be waiting to walk up on stage to shake hands with Portland's chief of police in front of TV cameras and an audience full of even more cops, I would have asked what you had been smoking.

But today I'm one of four people getting a Civilian Medal for Heroism from the city of Portland's police department. Me. Drew Lyle. Straight-C slacker. Except, I'm not sure I'm really those things anymore. Next month I start taking classes at Portland Community College to become a paramedic. While Gabie goes off to Stanford, probably not to become a doctor. Her parents seem to slowly be coming to terms with that idea. And the times we've all eaten dinner together, I think they like the questions I ask about the cases they've worked on. Hearing them talk is interesting in a way that none of my biology or health classes ever were.

The audience is clapping now as the police chief, Clayton Yee, hands plaques to the other two civilians getting medals. The two guys had been driving behind a semi that tried to avoid a stalled car. Instead it slid off the highway, overturned, and caught fire. They pulled the trucker from his burning rig. Now Yee and the two men pose for a few photos.

I'm wearing the same clothes I wore to Kayla's funeral. I find her in the audience and smile at her. She smiles back. Her hair's growing back, and her face has filled out. I've only seen her a few times this summer. She's never come back to work, except once to say good-bye.

Gabie's parents are here, sitting up front, looking proud. My mom isn't here. She's in rehab. She was given the choice between that and jail, and she chose rehab. Will it work? I don't know. The court allowed me to become an emancipated minor.

"Now I'd like to introduce you to Andrew Lyle and Gabriella Klug," Clayton Yee says. Hearing my full first name throws me off a little. Gabie has to poke me to remind me to walk up the stairs.

"Because of their selfless and courageous actions, without regard to their own personal safety, these two young people were able to save the life of their coworker, Kayla Cutler, and quite possibly prevent the deaths of many more young women. If these two young people hadn't stepped in to save their friend, who knows how many girls would have died in Ronald Hewett's basement?"

Camera flashes are going off, and a dozen guys are holding microphones out. We're not quite the sensation we were in the first few days after it happened, but it's still not unusual for me to see some mention of the story as one of the top news headlines on Web sites. And it still doesn't feel quite real.

I spot Sergeant Thayer in the audience. His arms are

crossed. I have a feeling that if it was up to him, we wouldn't be getting this award.

Sometimes I still have nightmares about it, about pulling that trigger and how Hewett fell back in a boneless sprawl. Like Flea Market Parade says, sometimes it feels like there's a criminal in my head. But then I think about Gabie and know I didn't have any choice.

Yee finishes speaking. The clapping swells, and I look at Gabie and smile. We both bow our heads a little and let the applause wash over us.

GOFISH

APRIL HENRY

© Randy Patten

What did you want to be when you grew up?
An ophthalmologist. Why? I have no idea. Maybe because it's so hard to spell.

When did you realize you wanted to be a writer?
Initially I thought about being a writer when I was nine or ten. Then I lost my courage and didn't find it again until I was about thirty.

What's your most embarrassing childhood memory?
People used to call me Ape, and I did a pretty good monkey impression. The trick is to put your tongue under your upper lip and scrunch up your nose while making chimp noises. Only now, looking back on it, I'm embarrassed to think about it.

What's your favorite childhood memory?
When I was ten, I asked for nothing but books for Christmas. After we unwrapped our presents, I went back into bed and read.

As a young person, who did you look up to most?

Roald Dahl, who wrote *Charlie and the Chocolate Factory*. I wrote him letters and sent him stories, and he sent me back a couple of postcards. I still have one that complimented my story about a six-foot-tall frog named Herman who loved peanut butter.

What was your favorite thing about school?

English and math, but I liked nearly all subjects. If life were like school, I would be a millionaire. Unfortunately for my bank account, real life and school only overlap to a certain extent.

What was your least favorite thing about school?

PE. I was the clumsiest person imaginable. I hurt my knee on the pommel horse, bruised my inner arm from wrist to elbow in archery, and sank when I was supposed to be swimming.

What were your hobbies as a kid? What are your hobbies now?

I read or hung out with my friends. We lived near a cool old cemetery and sometimes we would even go sledding or picnic there.

Now I run, read, and practice kajukenbo, a mixed marital art. We even spar—and I'm pretty good. If only my old PE teacher, Miss Fronk, could see me now.

What was your first job, and what was your "worst" job?

My first job was at a library in the children's section. I used to hide in the stacks and read Judy Blume when I was supposed to be shelving books.

My worst job was at a bank. A monkey who knew the alphabet could have done that job and would probably have had a better time.

How did you celebrate publishing your first book?

I stink at celebrating. I did buy a pair of earrings.

Where do you write your books?

On my couch, at the coffee shop, in the library, at the car fix-it place (where I am a lot).

What sparked your imagination for *The Night She Disappeared*?

The Night She Disappeared was inspired by a real, thirty-year-old case in which a pizza delivery girl went missing. In the book and in real life, the caller asked for a different girl first. For a long time, I wondered what it would be like to have been that other girl, to know that it could have been you who went missing. I finally decided to write about it.

What challenges do you face in the writing process, and how do you overcome them?

Deadlines are the biggest challenge. You just have to take them one day at a time.

Which of your characters is most like you?
All of my characters have a little bit of me in them. Even
the killers.

What makes you laugh out loud?
Failblog.org.

What do you do on a rainy day?
Rainy or overcast days are a part of everyday life in Portland. I do pretty much what I do on any day. The hardest
thing to do is to go out the door for a run when it's pouring. Once you get started, it's not so bad, but a GORE-TEX
jacket is essential.

What's your idea of fun?
Hanging out with my writing friends. Opening a book that
has been getting really great reviews. And sparring. I love
to spar. It makes me feel powerful to see a guy flinch.

What's your favorite song?
Right now I'm loving that same Adele song everyone else
is, "Rolling in the Deep."

Who is your favorite fictional character?
A guy named Rusty in a Scott Turow book. He is a liar and
a cheat, and as a reader you really like him. I'm still not
sure how Scott Turow pulled that off.

**What was your favorite book when you were a
kid? Do you have a favorite book now?**
I loved *The Silver Crown* by Robert C. O'Brien. I have read
so many books I don't have one favorite—I have

hundreds. *The Hunger Games* was great, as was *Life As We Knew It.*

What's your favorite TV show or movie?
I really like *Breaking Bad,* which is dark, dark, dark.

If you were stranded on a desert island, who would you want for company?
My teenage daughter. And a person who knew how to use the things you find on a desert island to build a boat.

If you could travel anywhere in the world, where would you go and what would you do?
I would spend a month in Italy looking at ruins and eating pasta.

If you could travel in time, where would you go and what would you do?
I'd like to see what the world would be like in two-hundred years' time.

What's the best advice you have ever received about writing?
Tenacity is as important as talent.

Do you ever get writer's block? What do you do to get back on track?
I force myself to write. You can't edit nothing. Or sometimes I'll jump ahead and write a part I was looking forward to writing.

What do you want readers to remember about your books?
That they were fun to read. And maybe the readers learned a little something. I do a lot of research.

What would you do if you ever stopped writing?
Die.

What do you like best about yourself?
If I see a need, I try to meet it.

Do you have any strange or funny habits? Did you when you were a kid?
When I'm bored, I catch myself making a cloverleaf tongue. My teenager has been able to make one since she was little, and once when I was bored I taught myself how. It's supposed to be a rare genetic trait, but I think if you can roll your tongue, you can learn how to do it.

What do you consider to be your greatest accomplishment?
My daughter is pretty cool. But she mostly did that on her own.

What do you wish you could do better?
Parallel park. I never really learned how, and now I drive around and around looking for spots I can pull into.

What would your readers be most surprised to learn about you?
Well, then it wouldn't be a surprise, would it? How about—I have one double-jointed thumb. (That's not giving too much away.)

"Take her out back and finish her off."

She doesn't know who she is. She doesn't know where she is, or why. All she knows when she comes to in a ransacked cabin is that there are two men arguing over whether or not to kill her. And that she must run.

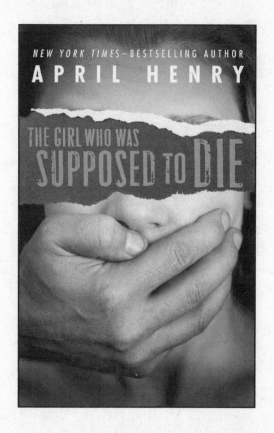

Turn the page for a peek at
April Henry's next nail-biting thriller,

THE GIRL WHO WAS SUPPOSED TO DIE.

CHAPTER 1
DAY 1, 4:51 P.M.
FINISH HER OFF

I wake up.

But wake up isn't quite right. That implies sleeping. A bed. A pillow.

I come to.

Instead of a pillow, my right cheek is pressed against something hard, rough, and gritty. A worn wood floor.

My mouth tastes like old pennies. Blood. With my eyes still closed, I gently touch my teeth with my tongue. One of them feels loose. The inside of my mouth is shredded and sore. My head aches and there's a faint buzzing in one ear.

And something is wrong with my left hand. The tips of my pinky and ring finger throb with every beat of my heart. The pain is sharp and red.

Two men are talking, their voices a low murmur. Something about no one coming for me. Something about it's too late.

I decide to keep my eyes closed. Not to move. I'm not sure I could anyway. It's not only my tooth that feels wrong.

Footsteps move closer to me. A shoe kicks me in the ribs. Not very hard. More like a nudge. Still, I don't allow myself to react. Through slitted eyes, I see two pairs of men's shoes. One pair of brown boots and one pair of red-brown dress shoes that shade to black on the toes. A distant part of me thinks the color is called oxblood.

"She doesn't know anything," a man says. He doesn't sound angry or even upset. It's a simple statement of fact.

I realize he's right. I don't know anything. What's wrong with me, where I am, who they are. And when I try to think about who I am, what I get is: nothing. A big gray hole. All I know for sure is that I must be in trouble.

"I need to get back to Portland and follow our leads there," the other man says. "You need to take care of things here. Take her out back and finish her off."

"But she's just a kid," the first man says. His tone is not quite so neutral now.

"A kid?" The second man's voice hardens. "If she talks to the cops, she could get us both sent to death row. It's either her or us. It's that simple." His footsteps move away from me. "Call me when you're done."

The other man nudges me with his foot again. A little harder this time.

Behind me, I hear a door open and close.

"Come on. Get up." With a sigh, he leans over and grabs me under my arms. Grunting, he hauls me up from behind. His breath smells bitter, like coffee. I try to keep my body limp, but when my left hand brushes the floor, the pain in my fingers is an electric shock. My legs stiffen and he pulls me to my feet.

"That's right," he says, nudging me forward while still holding me up. "We're going to take a little walk."

Since he already knows that I'm conscious, I figure I can open my eyes halfway. We're in what looks like a cabin, with knotty pine walls and a black wood-burning stove. Yellow stuffing spills from sliced cushions on an old plaid couch and a green high-backed chair. Books lie splayed below an emptied bookcase. Someone was obviously looking for something, but I don't know what, and I don't know if they found it. Past the red-and-white-checkered curtains lie nothing but fir trees.

With the guy's arm clamped around my shoulders, I stumble past a table with four wood chairs. One of them is turned away from the table. Ropes loosely encircle the arms. A pair of bloody pliers sits on the table next to what look like two silver-white chips mostly painted pink.

I look down at my limp left hand. Pink polish on three of the nails. The tips of the last two fingers are wet and red where nails used to be.

I think I know where I was before I ended up on the floor.

I keep every step small and shuffling so that he's half carrying me. It's not easy because he's not much bigger than me, maybe five foot nine. The guy mutters under his breath, but that's all. Maybe he doesn't want to get to where we are going any more than I do. The back door is about twenty feet away.

Outside, a car starts up and then drives away. The only

other sounds are the wind in the trees outside and the man grunting every now and then as he tries to make my body walk in a straight line.

Wherever we are, I think we're alone. It's just me and this guy. And once he manages to get me out the door, he'll follow instructions.

He'll finish me off.

Kill me.

CHAPTER 2
DAY 1, 4:54 P.M.
PLAYING DEAD

We keep walking toward the back door of the cabin. Except the guy holding me up is doing most of the walking. My left knee bangs into the nearest chair. I don't lift my feet, letting my toes drag on the ground. I'm trying to buy myself some time. Trying to figure out how to save myself. My half-closed eyes flick from side to side, looking for a weapon. Looking for anything that could help me. But there's no iron poker next to the wood stove, no knives on the counter, no old-fashioned black telephone on the wall. Just gaping drawers and emptied out cupboards and a big mess on the floor—cookie sheets and cans and dishtowels and boxes of cereal and crackers that have been upended and shaken empty.

He has to take one hand away from me to open the door. *"Don't act. Be,"* a voice whispers inside my head. I picture my consciousness dwindling. I let my body go limp, and slide from his grasp. It's tough to stay slack when my fingertips hit the rough wood. The pain arcs up my arm like I just stuck my fingers in a light socket. Still, I keep tumbling loosely to the floor it as if I'm completely out.

Playing dead. Hoping I won't *be* dead soon. Maybe if he thinks I'm unconscious, he'll let his guard down.

With a sigh, the man steps over me, and kicks the door open, letting in a wave of cold air. He leans down and rolls me over so that I'm face up again. It's so hard not to stiffen, especially as every bit of me feels tender and bruised, but I bite my tongue and try to remain loose. Then he grabs me under the arms and begins to drag me backward, grunting at every step. His chin brushes the top of my head.

He can't see my face. I wonder if that's a mistake. It will be easier to kill me if he doesn't have to look into my pleading eyes. Doesn't have to see my lips tremble as I beg for my life.

My feet thump over the sill. I open my eyes again. I see a worn earthen path stretching back to the cabin, my feet in blue Nike running shoes, my legs in skinny jeans. Reddish brown stains splotch the thighs. I wonder if the blood is only from my fingers.

I let my hands, even the broken one, trail along the ground. Under my fingertips, I feel cold earth, ridged with footprints, muddy in spots. A stick about as big around as one of my fingers. And then my good hand closes on a rock, small enough to fit into my palm, rounded on one side, with one sharp edge.

If this man has a gun—which seems more than

likely—the rock won't help me much. Even David had the help of a slingshot when he used a stone to kill Goliath.

The going is easier now. Pine trees surround us and my heels slide over copper-colored needles. I can't imagine this guy, who by now is breathing heavily, will drag me for miles and miles. Soon he'll drop me, take out his more-than-likely gun, and shoot me in the head. Or the heart. Or maybe both.

I'm going to die and I don't know why.

I don't even know who I am.

I wonder if he'll bother to bury me. Or maybe he'll just leave my body for whatever lives in these woods.

No! The thought is so fierce I have to clamp my lips together to keep from shouting it. I can't wait for *him* to choose what happens to me. I can't just wait for him to kill me.

He's dragging me past a small tree. I stick out one leg and hook my foot around the trunk. We jerk to a stop.

"Come on now." He sighs. "Let's not make this harder than it has to be."

He lifts me to reposition his grip. I manage to get my feet under me. He's so close his breath stirs the hair on the nape of my neck.

I don't know what I'm going to do until suddenly I'm doing it. My right elbow drives back like a piston, landing square in his belly. He grunts in an explosion of air and starts to fold up. The bottom of my right fist is already swinging down to hammer his groin. And then I swing my hand up, twisting it until the back of my fist hits him square in the face. Hard. And made even harder by the rock I hold in my hand. Under my knuckles, I feel the bridge of his nose crack.

I spin around to face him. His eyes are half closed in pain. Blood runs from his nose, red as paint. His right hand reaches out to grab me. My left hand rises, bent at the wrist like the neck of a crane, and knocks his hand away. Then my hand snaps back and claws down, fingers spread, my remaining fingernails digging into his cheeks, leaving furrows that immediately fill with blood. He cries out and puts his hands to his face.

Leaving his throat unprotected. I draw back my hand, my fingers close together and bent at the second knuckle. And I drive them into his throat as hard as I can.

And then he's lying flat on his back, not moving.

I'm not sure he's even breathing.

All my moves were automatic. I didn't have to think. Didn't have to remember anything.

Whoever I am, I already know how to do this.